WORKING FOR
THE MAN

Also by Ralph Dennis

The War Heist

The Hardman Series

Atlanta Deathwatch
The Charleston Knife is Back in Town
The Golden Girl And All
Pimp For The Dead
Down Among The Jocks
Murder Is Not An Odd Job
Working For The Man
The Deadly Cotton Heart
The One Dollar Rip-Off
Hump's First Case
The Last Of The Armageddon Wars
The Buy Back Blues

WORKING FOR THE MAN

RALPH DENNIS

BRASH
BOOKS

ISBN: 1-7324226-7-2
ISBN-13: 978-1-7324226-7-2

Published by
Brash Books, LLC
12120 State Line #253,
Leawood, Kansas 66209
www.brash-books.com

PUBLISHER'S NOTE

This book was originally published in 1974 and reflects the cultural and sexual attitudes, language, and politics of the period.

CHAPTER ONE

It was Sunday morning and I didn't want to get out of bed. That's not remarkable. I'm that way most Sundays, but this time there was a better reason. Beyond my bedroom window, I could hear the icy wind making those old radio serial sound effects like ghosts howling in the attic. It was almost enough to convince me to put my head under the covers and not come out until Monday.

Even in Atlanta Saturday night is a big night. Marcy and I had planned on an early dinner at The Abbey and a flick later, if we felt like it. We didn't even get out of my house. What had been a slow winter rain turned into an ice storm when the temperature dropped after dark. The trees became coated with sheets of ice and when the wind blew through the limbs they creaked, and now and then there was a popping explosion when a tree split somewhere off in the distance. A couple of times during the night I awakened to a blue-red flash on the skyline that meant a transformer had gone up.

The second hand on the electric clock still moved. That told me the electricity hadn't gone out during the night. Below, in the basement, the furnace chugged along with that "I can't make it, I can't make it" kind of rumble. And I believed it.

Up against me, blowing warm air in my face, Marcy said, "I've got two friends coming for lunch."

"Forget it," I said. "Nobody is going anywhere today."

"But..."

"I just hope there's something to eat in the house." I knew there was. It was just my way of confusing her mind.

"But … they'll be there at one o'clock."

"Don't whine."

"After I make breakfast, you'll have to drive me. I can't drive in this ice."

"Call them. I'll bet they've been trying to reach you for an hour to cancel out."

"You think so, Jim?"

"Sure, and I know one thing more. Your reputation is ruined. Any girl who's not home on Sunday morning must be out screwing." I rolled toward the night table and grabbed the phone. I lifted it over me and dropped it in her hands. "Call them."

I was asleep by the time she'd dialed the first number.

The bed was empty when I came out of the dark deep, drawn, I guess, by the smell of frying salty country ham and the flour-butter scent of homemade biscuits. And floating over all that, waves of perking coffee.

"You were right." Marcy, wearing jeans and one of my old shirts, dumped a pan of biscuits into a bread basket and pushed it toward me. "Ethel Ann said she'd been trying to reach me."

"She giggle about your love life?" I broke open a biscuit, buttered it, and placed a hunk of ham in the middle. It was the real country ham. Dark and hard and salty as sea water.

"And Ruth said her electricity is off and she'd have to stay at her mother's until it comes back on."

I chewed on the ham biscuit. After I choked it down, I said, "Glad you didn't go charging out?"

"Of course."

She brought the coffee pot around the table and refilled my cup. I put up an arm and wrapped it around her hips. She's a tall girl. Close to her, I could smell the warm bed scent of her. It was better than any perfume.

It had worked out the way I'd wanted it to. I didn't much like driving on ice either.

It was almost one in the afternoon before the Sunday paper got delivered. I was thawing it out in the living room when the phone rang in the bedroom. Marcy was changing the sheets and making the bed. I waited until she called me.

"It's for you, Jim."

"It ought to be. It's my house." I patted her on the rump on the way past her. "Yeah?" I said into the receiver.

"The Man wants to see you."

"Who is this?"

"It don't matter."

I sat on the edge of the bed and turned and got a disapproving look from Marcy. "Let me talk to him."

"He can't come right now. He's in his bath."

"What does he want to see me about?"

There was a hesitation. The caller wasn't used to that kind of question. The Man was a black ex-pimp who worked his way up to become the top man in the rackets in Atlanta. A lot of clout and power. When he spoke and when he hooked a finger at you, your a-hole tightened and you were supposed to come running. "You get the morning paper, Hardman?"

"A few minutes ago."

"Read it yet?"

"Just the headlines on the front page."

"I'll hold. You read about the killing on page 5A."

I put the receiver aside and found the A section in the living room. I flipped over to page 5 on my way back into the bedroom. There was a small piece on the bottom left of the page, next to a big ad for Davison's Department Store.

3

Torture Murder of Gambler Probed

I read it through once. A known gambler named John B. Kent had been found in his apartment at the Starlight Estates by the resident manager. He'd been tortured and killed. Kent had a number of arrests in his past, all related to gambling activities. He was 60 and unmarried. The police had no leads but they were questioning tenants at the Starlight Estates.

I put the paper aside. "So what? I've read it and I don't know anything about him."

"But you know old Ronny?"

"Sure." I felt the first brush of a chill.

"Kent was old Ronny."

"How—?"

"He fought under that name when he was young. Ronny Gellin. And he used his real name after that."

I remembered. When he'd been fighting it had been the time of the fast, young Jewish welters and lightweights. A good reason for taking the name.

"I knew him then," I said. And I could remember the lumpy scar tissue around his eyes and the way both ears were.

"The Man wants to talk to you about him. You willing?"

"I don't want to drive in this crap."

At the foot of the bed, tucking in the blankets, Marcy laughed at me.

"You alone?"

"No."

"A driver will pick you up in twenty minutes."

He hung up. I walked around the bed to the closet and started dressing. "I've got to go out."

"Why, Jim?"

"It's important." I picked warm clothing. A pair of heavy tweed slacks and a wool shirt I wore when the weather got bad. When I got that far, I found a pair of wool socks and unclipped the shoetrees from the heavy English shoes I'd bought a few months back. "I'll call you in an hour if it looks like I can't come right back home."

"What is it, Jim?"

"A man I knew is dead and I owed him. Now somebody wants to talk to me about him and I think I'd better listen."

"I might not be here when you get back. I might call a cab."

"I can't help it." I buttoned up a cardigan and unzipped the bag that covered my heavy topcoat.

"But I thought we were just going to loaf around all day."

"I thought so too." I didn't even look at the shoebox in the back of the closet. That was where I kept my spare cash and my .38 Police Positive. I wouldn't need it and The Man might not appreciate it if I came over carrying iron.

On the way back into the living room I stopped and put an arm around her. I could feel her back stiffen. "I'll be back as soon as I can."

"If I'm here."

"Come on, Marcy. I wouldn't go out if I could help it." I backed away from her and put on the topcoat. It smelled of a summer in the closet. "Look, there's stuff to make a jambalaya in the refrigerator. You stew up the sauce and cook the rice and the shrimp. I'll be back to help you put it together."

"And you'll tell me what it's about?"

"As soon as I know myself."

Fifteen minutes later I heard the tire chains on the road. It was the only car moving out there. I stood by the driveway and waited until the black LTD slowed to a stop. There were two young blacks in the front seat. Hard dudes I didn't know. It didn't mean anything. There was always a big turnover among the soldiers who worked for The Man. Either you made it or you got culled.

They didn't say anything to me and I didn't feel like talking anyway. I opened the back door and got in. On the drive back into town I could see the damage from the storm. Some trees were down and the overpasses were slick. It was hard driving for the black behind the wheel. He handled the ice well, like he'd lived a time up north or had lessons.

After a few minutes I leaned back in the seat and closed my eyes.

About twenty years had passed since I first met Ronny. It had been right after the Korean War and I'd been mustered out in Atlanta. I had some cash put aside and I was full of piss and pickle juice. It was before I decided to go on the Force. I was drinking and chasing tail and hanging around the fringes of the dark side of the town. Where the nightcrawlers and the meat-eaters were.

One night I got into a poker game. Ronny was one of the six in the game but I didn't know him then. He was about forty, a dapper little man, not more than a hundred and forty pounds. Trim, not like he was later when the fat settled on him. Dressed in a dark brown suit with a vest and a red tie with the knot tight and square under his Adam's apple. Clean French cuffs showing about a half inch beyond his jacket sleeve. The dull wink of small gold nuggets on his cuff links. His trademark, I learned later. He'd won them off a tapped-out gambler in a game that ran coast to coast, three days on a train.

I didn't belong in the game. I should have known that. Still, I thought I was hard ass of the year and hadn't I learned to play cards with the sharp guys in Japan and Korea? As it turned out I couldn't have been more wrong.

If I'd known as much about cards as I thought I did, it wouldn't have taken two hours to figure out what was going on. I'd have noticed how Ronny was playing it. Tight, never in unless he had the cards.

Six of us in the game. Ronny and me and two other small-timers who didn't belong either and the two who were working the game for all it was worth. Those two, the way they acted toward each other, you'd have thought they'd just met.

I was about four hundred down before I got the feeling I was being had. I was getting good cards and betting them and I'd take a pot now and then, the small ones. When the pot was big and I had some of the right cards, enough to stay in, either Frank, the hard dark guy, or Ernie, the small pale dude with red hair, kept bumping the bet up and up. And usually one or the other edged me by a red hair or two. It was the same with the two other small-timers. Looking back on it, I've always wondered why Ronny stayed in the game at all. Unless, after he understood what was going on, he decided to see how it would end up.

Frank and Ernie were damned good mechanics, up with the best of them, and I might have written it off as a bad run of cards if I hadn't lost on two straight pots. Ernie won the first one and when he put down his cards and said, "Three aces," Frank reached out and spread the bunched cards. The next hand Frank won with a full house and when he placed his cards they were packed and Ernie leaned over to spread them out and show them. It was all very casual, without a bad beat to it, but it finally got past the thick part of my skull.

Young then, I didn't have a lot of cool in the way I handled it. I cleared my throat, feeling the choking anger there, and said, "From now on, unless you're a cripple, spread your own hand."

The table got quiet. Across from me, Ronny pushed his cards toward the center of the table and edged his chair away. The two small-timers did the same. Frank and Ernie didn't move. Frank looked at me, level and hard, and said, "Close it out for the night, kid. No use getting a rep as a bad loser."

"I lose well," I told him, "when I really lose."

Ernie was on my left. He was small and I thought I could handle him if it went that far. I watched him from the corner of my eye. My real attention was on Frank. If there was any danger it would come from him.

Ronny stood up slowly. He got a cigarette from the pack on the table and lit it with a match from a book beside it. He blew a long stream of smoke toward me.

Ernie said, "You saying something about the game?"

I didn't look directly at him. "The game is rank and you know it."

I heard the click then. Frank had one hand under the table. I didn't have to see it to know what he was holding. A switchblade knife, the cutting edge out now.

Sweating. I was a few seconds from having to hold my guts in with both hands. It wasn't a pleasant thought. Knives aren't kind to most people and I wasn't any different.

Ronny drew on his cigarette. It wasn't a steady puff-puff but enough so that the coal on the end of the cigarette looked hard and red.

"I guess you're just a born loser." Frank eased his chair back. He leaned forward slightly and got his feet under him. He was going to get to his feet and then come around the table after me. He didn't get that far. Ronny took the cigarette out of his mouth, flicked the ash away, and rammed the hot coal into the back of Frank's neck. It must have hurt like hell.

Frank yelled, "God dammit," and turned on Ronny. The knife was coming up above the table when Ronny one-punched him. It was a short right that didn't travel more than about five or six inches. Frank went down backwards, taking the chair with him.

That left Ernie. Just to be sure there were no more surprises, any rabbit-in-the-hat knives, I leaned in and hit Ernie on the side of the neck as hard as I could.

After that, we wrote *end* on the game. While the two small-timers beat and kicked Frank and Ernie in one corner of the room, Ronny and I split up the money. I got back my four hundred and Ronny was about a hundred ahead for the night.

"They were H-O-ing you," Ronny said at the bar down the street from the hotel. He was drinking Jack Daniels with water on the side. I sipped a draft.

"Good at it?"

Ronny smiled. "Good enough. I think they might have gotten away with it if they hadn't been greedy."

"You mean, showing it to me two times in a row?"

"That was it." He lifted a hand from under the table and reached out toward me. The back of his hand was to me and I couldn't see anything. He touched the table top and moved the hand away. There was a Queen lying on the table.

"You too?"

"I know the game." He tossed back the shot of Daniels and followed it with a swallow of water. "That last game you had what?"

"Trip fours."

"After the draw Frank had two pairs. Jacks and tens." He lifted a hand and rubbed four fingers across his eyes. "You see that?"

"What?"

He did it again. The same gesture like he was rubbing smoke out of his eyes. "That's how Frank asked the question. Do you have a Jack?" Ronny rapped the table top with a balled fist. "That was Ernie's answer. Yes."

"Got it." I felt young and stupid.

"Frank drops his fifth card on the discards while seeming to be pushing them away. Now he's got just four cards, the Jacks and the tens. They whipsaw you some with the raises. And when it's show time, Frank calls his hand and places it on the table bunched." Ronny, casual and easy, the way Ernie had done it, reached out and made the gesture that would spread the cards. I didn't see him do it, but when he moved his hand away there was a card on the table. It wasn't a Jack but I could see how Ernie had supplied Frank with the third Jack that tied up his full house.

We had another drink and Ronny was ready to leave. I don't remember much of what we talked about over that second drink. Just the last thing he said. "One thing about calling somebody in a game like that. You ought to be standing up when you do it and you ought to have something in your hand."

Now he was dead and for some reason The Man had an interest in it. It was odd. As far as I knew they hadn't known each other.

The Man hadn't moved. It was still the same auto parts store with the boarded-up front. Flaking paint that advertised parts for cars they didn't build any more. A gravel parking lot in back. A locked door that led into a spotlessly clean stairwell. Up those stairs to a landing and another locked door. Behind this door was the apartment where The Man lived.

One of the last times I'd been at The Man's place I'd been doing a job for him and there was a dead black man at the bottom of the stairs and the body of a white on the landing. The door and the apartment beyond had been shot all to hell. It had been a try on The Man.

At the landing, without the two blacks saying anything, I opened my topcoat. One of them leaned in and patted me down. When he was satisfied I wasn't carrying anything, he stepped away and gave the other black a short nod. That one reached past me and rapped on the door.

Someone opened the door and we walked in. A white sofa and a coffee table with a brass top were over to the right. In the center of the room, taking up most of the space, was a circular bar with about a twenty-year supply of booze. The last time I saw the bar it was heavy brass and a burp gun had stitched some special decorations across it. Now the brass was replaced by ceramic tile in a kind of floral design of greens and blues and reds. One thing you could say about The Man: he had no taste at all.

Past the bar was the kitchen-dining room. Off to the right a door led to the bedroom. That door was closed and since I didn't see The Man anywhere, I made my guess that he was still dressing.

The two blacks who escorted me stood in the doorway that led to the stairs. "We're going to get something to eat. Ought to be back in half an hour or so."

The black bodyguard who had let us in, and who carried a 12-gauge pumpgun under one arm, nodded and said, "No more than forty-five."

After the door closed behind them, we listened to the clatter on the stairs and looked at each other. He was slim and wiry, with that odd coloring you see now and then among blacks. His hair had a kind of red tint to it and his pale skin had the freckling that, when I was a kid, we'd thought that meant that he had a lot of white blood in him.

"He said to fix you a drink." He turned and placed the pump-gun on the bar and dipped under the opening and came up on the other side of the counter.

"Best cognac you've got." I could still feel the chill from the ride and from the wind that blew across the parking lot.

"I don't know which one is best." While I watched, he lined up the brands on the bar. Martell, Remy Martin, Bisquit, Hennessy and a brand of armagnac I didn't know. When I didn't choose from that group, he added a bottle of 5-star Metaxa.

"Anything else?"

A moment of hesitation and he reached low behind the bar and lifted out a bottle of twenty-year-old Hines. I grinned at him and nodded. "About a handful of that."

"It's what he drinks," he said, swinging his head toward the bedroom door. When he turned back, he placed a large snifter on the bar and poured about three knuckles of cognac into it. "Guess it must be good."

I threw down about half the shot and felt the warmth spread all the way down to my toes. I placed the snifter back on the bar and nodded and he refilled it up to the wet line.

A few minutes later, The Man came in from the bedroom.

The last couple of years didn't show on him. Still hard as black stone, graceful and slim. Dressed now in gray flared slacks and a gold-colored smoking jacket.

"Did you find anything worth drinking, Hardman?"

I nodded at the bar. The young black had put away all the bottles except for the Hines. One look at the bottle and The Man grinned. "I'm glad you could come and visit," he said to me.

"If you weren't in, I'd have left my calling card."

The black brought The Man a snifter of the Hines. Backing away, the black said, "Freddie and Vince went to eat."

"Fine." The Man sat on the sofa but he kept his distance.

"Ought to be back in forty minutes or so."

The Man lifted his nose out of the snifter. "Wait on the landing."

"Sure." The young black lifted the pumpgun from the bar and went out and closed the door behind him. I knew the kind of dudes that The Man hired. Going out in the cold wasn't anything. If he'd told them to, they'd have jumped into a vat of hot chicken fat.

"I was right to think you knew old Ronny?"

"I knew him. I might even have owed him."

"He told me once," The Man said. "That card game all those years ago."

"That was the one."

"His death bother you?"

I said, "Old men die."

"And the way he died?"

"It sounded messy."

"You didn't see much of him the last few years, did you?"

No reason to lie. "I saw him at a Falcon game a couple of years ago. Saw him at three or four Braves games last summer."

"You know he was tapped-out?"

"Him?" It didn't make sense. "He had half the money in town."

"Not the last two or three years," The Man said. "His stomach started bothering him and he lost his nerve."

"That doesn't sound like him."

"You laugh if I told you he'd been working for me the last year or so?"

I said, "I'm not laughing."

"It wasn't charity. Not exactly. He was keeping some books for me."

A comedown of sorts. "He had a good head for figures."

"It was *sub rosa*."

"You taking Latin now?"

"I knew about it and he knew about it. Nobody else. Not even my best boys knew about it. Once a week I'd drop off a ledger and a folder full of notes on my transactions. They were coded to some degree. A couple of days later he'd call me and I'd pick up the ledger and the folder. I'd burn the notes and lock the ledger away."

I could see the shape of it. "When did you drop off the ledger and the rough data this week?"

"Friday." He didn't blink.

"So normally you'd hear from him on Monday?"

"Or late Sunday."

"And now the ledger is missing?"

"That's what my sources tell me."

"How damaging is it?" I lifted the snifter and sipped at it.

"The ledger? Not at all unless you can read the code. This symbol stands for one bagman and that one for another bagman."

"Who'd want the ledger?"

"The locals or the Feds."

I shook my head. "Murder's not their way. Bug your phone or buy your brother, that's their thing."

"You don't understand, Hardman." He cupped his hands around the snifter and warmed the cognac. "I said the locals and the Feds would like to have the ledger. I didn't say they had it."

"Who then?"

"I don't know." He stood up and carried his snifter to the bar. He tipped the bottle of Hines and added a few drops to his glass. "I've got something I want you to hear." He pointed toward the kitchen-dining room.

I followed him.

In the back, left corner there was something that wasn't there the last time I was in the apartment. Next to the phone there was a tape recorder.

"When I'm asleep or out, a switch throws all the incoming calls onto the recorder. There's always somebody here. They take the calls and what's said is recorded, just in case there's some doubt about what's said."

"You having trouble finding good boys these days? Ones who can take messages?"

He ignored me. He turned on the machine and punched down the "Play" button.

"Hello."

"This is Vince answering the phone," The Man said.

"I want to speak to The Man." The voice was that of a man, but one with a mouthful of mush.

"Nobody by that name here."

"And up you too, Charlie. Put him on the phone."

"Who is this?"

"That doesn't matter. You tell him I've got the ledger."

"What ledger is that?"

"It's black. It's covered with leatherette. About six inches wide and twelve inches high."

I turned to The Man. "It's the right one," he said.

"I don't know anything about a ledger."

"*Dumb fucking burr-head. I'll call back at eleven when The Man is there. You make sure he's there.*"

The line went dead. The Man punched the "Stop" button.

"What time did the call come in?"

"About eight this morning. Vince got me up and I listened to the tape."

"You know the time Ronny was killed?"

"No way I could have. It wasn't on the late news last night and since nobody, not even my sources, knew that Ronny was keeping books for me, there wasn't any reason for them to call me."

"So you made a few calls. Ronny didn't answer. You called somebody close to the police and you found out Ronny was dead and there wasn't a ledger at his apartment."

"That's it." He punched the "Play" button. "This call came in at eleven on the dot."

"*Hello.*" I could recognize The Man's voice.

"*You always sleep this late?*"

"*Who is this?*"

"*The man who has the ledger.*"

"*What do you want?*"

"*Fifty thousand dollars.*"

"*For what?*"

"*Wake up.*" The man with the mush in his mouth sounded irritated. "*I want fifty thousand for the ledger.*"

"*It's not worth that.*"

"*Today's bargain day. It's worth more than fifty grand and you know it.*"

"*Not to me.*"

"*I know somebody who'll pay a finder's fee.*"

"*Who?*"

"*The Feds. The I.R.S.*"

"*All right,*" The Man said. "*It's worth that much to me.*"

I looked at The Man. His mouth was twisted. He didn't like me hearing him give in that easy.

"I want it in tens and twenties."

"How and when?"

"I don't want it delivered by you or your boys. I can't see you or them in the dark."

"Who then?"

"This guy in town did some work for you once. Jim Hardman. The slow, fat one."

"I know him."

"Get the money together. Pack it in a bag. Get it to Hardman. He holds it until I call him and give him instructions."

"When?"

"Later today."

"I can't get it together by then. The banks are closed."

"Monday afternoon?"

"All right."

"Old money," mushmouth said.

"How do I know you'll turn over the ledger?"

"You don't."

A click. The line was dead. The Man hit the "Stop" button. I turned and walked back into the living room. On my way past the bar, I tapped the Hines bottle. I needed something to get the sour taste out of my mouth. I slumped down on the sofa and lit a cigarette and nibbled at the cognac. What bothered me was that during the whole conversation The Man hadn't said a thing about Ronny's killing.

The Man eased in and stood with one hip against the bar.

"You had me fooled there for a minute," I said. "I thought you gave a shit about Ronny."

"I do," The Man said. "I cared enough about him to pay him a couple of grand a month. It was pride money. It left him his pride." I could feel the hard sting of his anger. "Where were you,

Hardman, when his nerve went and he lost his stash and he was living on canned soup?"

"All he had to do was ask me."

"You know goddam well he wouldn't do that. He didn't with me and he wouldn't with you. The big difference was that I found out he needed help and I did something about it. I asked him to do me some favors and every time I picked up the ledger at his place, I left him an envelope with five bills in it on his john seat. I cared enough not to hand him the money. Not to seem to be buying him."

"All right." I ground out the cigarette and burned a couple of fingertips doing it. I felt shaky. Head down, I had a realization about The Man. He hadn't sent his bodyguard out to the landing because he didn't want him to hear about the ledger. He probably already knew. No, it was because The Man knew he was going to have some trouble convincing me. He needed me and to get me he'd have to show the soft part of him. He could show it to me and I'd understand. His boys wouldn't. They'd see it as weakness.

"What now?"

"First things first," The Man said. "I want that ledger back."

"Tell me about second things."

He smiled then. It had about as much humor in it as rank sour vomit had perfume. "I want his ass on a plank."

"The third thing," I said, "is if I do this, I might be the one who ends up on the plank."

"That's the risk."

"And it bothered you?"

"You want me to lie to you?"

I shook my head at him. "But it'll cost you a thousand."

"If that's what it takes."

"And how I handle it is up to me?"

"After you get the ledger," he said. "After the ledger is safe."

"Agreed."

"I'll send the money around to you tomorrow, right after the banks open."

I stood up. "You'd better give me the thousand now. I might not be around to collect it later."

He went into the bedroom and closed the door behind him. I walked over to the door to the stairs and pulled it open. The bodyguard and the other two blacks were seated on the stairs, passing a thick joint around in a circle.

"Warm up the car. I'm about ready to leave."

The black who was lipping the joint looked like he wanted to tip it back into his mouth and swallow it. I shook my head at him and closed the door between us.

The Man came back and counted the thousand out into my hand. In bright new hundreds.

At my house the sauce for the jambalaya was ready. The rice was done and the shrimp had been boiled. Marcy cubed the ham while I told her an edited version of my meeting with The Man.

Once, when her back was to me, I grabbed the Tabasco bottle from the shelf and dripped in another dozen or so drops. I like the sauce hot and Marcy doesn't.

I figured I might as well live it up while I could.

CHAPTER TWO

B y morning the ice was melting on the roads.
After a cup of coffee, Marcy decided that she could man-
age the slush. I saw her off and then walked around the house to
the backyard. There wasn't any real damage from the ice storm.
Some pruning of dead limbs. Off in the distance, in the yard that
butted up against the back of mine, an oak tree had toppled from
the weight of the ice, the cluster of roots sticking up raw and clot-
ted with red mud.

I called Hump at nine. "Busy?"

"At nine in the morning?"

"Got us a job. Five bills in it for you."

"I could use it. Christmas is coming."

He was at my place an hour later when The Man's soldiers
brought the fifty thousand by and left it with me. It was in an old
gym bag that smelled of dirty socks and jock straps.

Hump and I have been doing odd jobs for a couple of years. He's
a lot like me. Shiftless and lazy, Marcy would say. Doesn't want
a nine-to-five job. Thinks those people who keep bubbling about
how much they love their jobs are a step and a half from the
funny farm.

We're alike up to there. Then it splits. I'm going toward forty-
three a bit too fast to suit me. I'm slow and pudgy and I get a sun-
burn the first time I stand in the sun more than ten minutes. He's

a bit past thirty and somewhere between 6 foot 6 inches and 6 foot 7 inches and the last time I saw him on the scales at the S&W cafeteria downtown on Peachtree the needle stopped at 270 and some ounces. He's also midnight down in the coal mine black.

When I think about it, I have to admit it's a strange relationship. Hump doesn't like whites much and sometimes I think he's bothered because some people misunderstand and think he's my "boy," that he works for me. Not so. He's his own man. And we cut the pie right down the middle when there's a pie to cut.

Back a few years ago, I was a cop here in Atlanta. That soured and I left before they could ask me to leave. Back around the same time, Hump was a damned good defensive end with Cleveland, a top one and All-Pro the year before he tore up a knee. The knee didn't get back a hundred percent and he quit. He'd slowed and he knew he couldn't hack it any more. Even now, his slow is about five steps faster than anybody's I know.

What's left for him in the straight world doesn't appeal much to him. And what's left to me, with my slightly tainted rep, doesn't roll me out of bed in the morning, laughing and giggling. That's the circle: we're back to what we have in common.

Now we do odd jobs. Anything that pays. Anything that stops this side of killing. Or mugging for booze money. Or robbing banks.

They kept us waiting. Maybe it was to make the stew taste better. Or it might have been designed to put me on edge. The call came at six.

"Hardman?" It was the same voice, the mushmouth quality I'd heard on the tape.

"Yeah."

"Got the cash?"

"I've got it."

"Listen close. I'll say it one time. I want you to drive over to Techwood and park in front of the Omni."

The Omni is the crushed *egg* carton that's made of steel and is supposed to turn into a beautiful work of art after the steel rusts and the patina develops. The Hawks and the Flames play their home games there. It's also booked for everything from rock shows to fashion parades. The only event that hasn't been booked there is an exhibition of nude women wrestling in tubs of mud.

"When?"

"Eight o'clock."

"You want me to be at the Omni at eight on the dot?"

"No, you leave your house exactly at eight and drive straight to the Omni."

"All right."

"You'll get the rest of the instructions there."

"It's your ballgame."

"And come alone and no iron."

He hung up.

Hump left at six-thirty. It would be a long wait in bad weather. I wanted him in position at least an hour before I arrived at the Omni and I wanted him out of the house before the tail showed up. That was the way we figured it. Because they'd insisted I not leave the house with the money until eight, we realized that I'd probably be followed. I guessed that it would be a loose tail that would "show" any friends of mine who tagged along.

Before Hump left, I loaned him a scarf and fixed him a thermos of coffee. As a last kindly thought, I dug out an old plastic flask and filled it with Stock, the Italian vermouth, out of a part of a bottle I had from last winter.

I was ready to leave a few minutes before eight. I'd spent some time considering the .38 P.P. that I keep packed away in a shoebox in my closet. No, if I had to stand a frisk, I didn't want to give them any ideas or a weapon to use on me. I settled for the slapjack. I rolled up the sleeve on my left arm and taped the slapjack to the inside of my forearm with adhesive tape. It was uncomfortable, the cuff button wouldn't reach and when I had my coat on, I felt like I'd stuffed a broomstick up my sleeve. So much for sneaky ideas. If I had to use it, if I had to reach up there and tear the tape away, a lot of hair and roots would come with it.

At exactly eight, I picked up the battered old gym bag and walked out of the house.

About twenty minutes later, I was on Techwood heading toward the Omni. From a distance I could see that it was dark. No show, no game this night. Techwood was almost deserted. Until the rest of the area was developed, there wasn't not much reason to use that stretch of the Drive. No headlights came toward me and only a faint dim light that might have been a car's lights were behind me.

I pulled up to the curb in front of the Omni and waited.

Seconds later, headlights raked the back window, lighting me up and the inside of the car. A late model black Ford ran up behind me and swerved and passed me at the last second. I waited for it to swing into my headlights. There was one long blast from the Ford's horn, just before it edged into the beam of my lights. No chance of getting the tag numbers. The license plate was smeared, probably with mud.

I hadn't been told to follow the car or respond to any signal from a car horn, so I waited. About half a minute later, I heard footsteps out on the walk coming from the direction of the Omni. When the footsteps died, I heard a tapping on the window next to the curb. I slid over and rolled down the window.

It was a black kid. I put his age at twelve or thirteen. The whites of his eyes were wide and ghostly against his black skin. His breath hissed out at me, frosting the top of the rolled-down window.

"You 'sposed to go down those steps there. The steps that goes down to the underground garage."

"Who are you?" I reached out and grabbed for his shoulder. He backed away.

"You 'sposed to," he said again. He whirled and ran toward the Omni, toward the darkness there. He was moving fast. The best day I ever had, I couldn't have caught him.

Now I regretted I hadn't brought the iron. They'd fooled me. It wasn't the way I'd figured it. I'd thought I'd be met at the Omni, frisked, and driven somewhere else where the exchange would take place. Whoever it was, that craphead, he was a couple of steps ahead of me.

I reached up my left sleeve and tore the tape free. I shook the slapjack out and dropped it into my right topcoat pocket. The gym bag in my left hand, I got out of the car and walked toward the Omni.

The stairwell was the real bottleneck of the Omni design. There was plenty of parking space below and there were a number of entrances that led into the garage. No trouble there. But then you had to climb those stairs to go under Techwood and come up near the sports complex. The stairwell was only about three people wide and it was hell in there just before a game or just after.

I stopped at the mouth of the stairs. It was dark down below. No light showed. Either the Omni management saved on the lights when there wasn't an event scheduled or somebody had taken the trouble to knock them out.

"Hardman?" It was the voice I'd heard before.

"It's me."

"Alone?"

"You heard the one horn signal." It was a guess.

"Smartass." A single pencil point of light switched on. It was below me, about where I thought the landing was. From the thin beam I decided that the light probably came from a flashlight that had its lens covered except for a spot in the center about the size of a fingertip. The narrow beam wagged up the stairs toward me.

"Down here, Hardman."

"Show me the ledger." Hand deep in my topcoat pocket, I gripped the slapjack handle.

Leather soles shifted beyond the light at a distance. Not the shoes of the man with the light. Sand and grit grinding as he moved. The pencil head of light swung away from me. The man with the flashlight was turning. Perhaps to reach for the ledger. I was right. The ledger was there, the black leatherette cover shining in the light.

At least two men down there.

"Bring the money down, Hardman."

"No."

"You got the money?"

"I've got it."

"Bring it down."

"Not a fucking chance."

The impatience was there, crackling between us. "Where do you want it, Hardman? In the leg or the gut?"

"Put the ledger on the steps halfway up to me."

"And you'll do what?"

"I'll throw the money down to you."

"Do it." It was another man, not the mushmouth one. The sound of someone using an unnatural voice, forced and raspy.

The light moved forward. The man placed the ledger on the steps and played the light across it. "The money, Hardman."

"Here." I tossed the bag at him. I threw it as hard as I could, wanting to get it past him. The light beam whirled away from the step where the ledger was.

"Bastard."

"Watch that light." Alarm, panic, in the same strained and forced voice.

He switched the light off. I leaned forward, grabbed the handrail and went down the steps on my tiptoes. Below me they'd found the bag. I heard it unzip. Not much time. I reached down. If I'd charted it right in my mind the ledger would be there. Fingers running along the front edge of the step. A few more inches and I had it. I grabbed the ledger and backed away. Before I reached the mouth of the stairwell the light went on, jammed down into the gym bag. A count of two or three and I could feel the top of the handrail. Just then the light jerked away from the bag and raked along the wall until it wagged up the steps.

"It's all there," I said. Turning, my feet braced, I sailed the ledger across the courtyard in a kind of fluttering discus shot.

The light reached the toes of my shoes and then tilted once more. He was searching for the ledger. "Where is it?"

"You got the money. I got the ledger. That was the deal."

"Next time, Hardman."

"How about right now?"

"Next time."

The light tracing their way down the stairwell, around an elbow and out of sight. The footsteps going away. Down to the underground parking. A heavy step and a light one. A big man and a small one, maybe.

I wasn't about to follow them. I went looking for the ledger. I found it spread out, the sheets fluttering in the wind. I was putting it under my arm when I heard running. Someone heading for me. I took out the slapjack and waited.

"Jim?" It was Hump.

"Here."

"You all right?"

"I got the ledger. Where're you parked?"

"On Forsyth," he said. "I walked over."

"What you been doing?"

"Chasing some kid." I could hear the shuddering breath as he tried to back it down to normal.

I laughed, the tension of the last few minutes gone in one big hoot. "Lost a step, huh?"

"That kid, he does a nine-one hundred."

We turned and walked to my car. Techwood Drive, as far as I could see in both directions, seemed swept clean by the icy wind.

"You look at it?"

Hump and I were seated on the white sofa. The Man stood at the bar, the ledger open in front of him.

"I looked," I said. "It didn't make any sense to me."

"That's the idea." He slammed the ledger shut and brought a new bottle of Hines over and tipped a bit into each of our glasses. "It worked out pretty well."

I took a sip from the snifter and rolled it around on my tongue. I eyed him hard over the rim. "You look in the back of the ledger?"

"No."

"Look," I said. It was bad news and it wasn't my business to be the bad news messenger. I'd hoped he'd find it himself.

He placed the Hines bottle on the bar and flipped the ledger open. It opened to where the paperclip was. He unclipped the sheet and unfolded it. I didn't need to look it over. I'd already had the sick feeling that went with it. The sheet was a xerox copy of pages 19 and 20 of the ledger.

"Goddam it." He hammered his clenched fist on the bar top.

"It's not over yet," I said. "That was the first payment."

"No more payments," he shouted. "Not another fucking dime."

"How're you going to work it?"

"I'm going to hire you two."

Hump shook his head. "I don't like working for you."

"The thing tonight," I said, "I did it so I could get close to whoever killed Ronny."

"And for the thousand dollars," The Man said.

That was too simple. "If you sent me for a newspaper it would cost you a hundred."

"Ten thousand. Half of it right now and the other half when I'm sure there are no more copies of this thing floating around out there."

I just looked at him.

He turned to Hump. "You can use some cash, can't you? Now—"

Hump reached up and picked at his nose. "The fat man knows his own mind."

"You never do anything right," I said to The Man. "You've got it ass-backwards."

"How?"

"What you really want to hire me to do is find out who killed Ronny. Right?"

The Man chewed his lip.

I stood up and waved a hand at Hump. He tossed back the rest of the cognac and whistled to himself as the heat bounced off his stomach. I waited until Hump was standing. "You'd better get another fifty thou together. They'll be back in a week or so."

"Okay, your way, Hardman. But my question is: what do I get out of it?"

It didn't take but two fingers to tick it off for him. "I want to find out who killed Ronny. That's one. If I run into the xerox copies they go to you. That's two."

"If it's the only way?"

"It's the only way."

Before we left The Man's apartment, we split the five thousand right down the middle. The Man watched us with sleepy eyes. Behind the sleep, the anger was real and rank and bitter as the center of a Carter's Little Liver pill.

CHAPTER THREE

The power saws were ripping and whining when I got out of bed the next morning. The cleanup was underway after the ice storm. I'd have slept longer but with the noise, I felt I'd awaken right in the middle of one of those old WWII movies where the Seabees had to build a complete airstrip in less than 24 hours.

It was early. I tried Art Maloney at his house and found him about three steps away from his bed. As long as I'd known him, and especially since he'd moved to Homicide, he liked working nights. Maybe for a good practicing Catholic, it's a form of birth control.

His tongue sounded thick, swollen, perhaps from too many cigarettes and too much coffee during the long night. "What's wrong, Jim? You got some trouble? I told you to stop hanging around schoolyards until you had that zipper fixed."

"I didn't call you for your jokes," I said. I waited a beat. "That is a joke, isn't it?"

"All right, Jim. What is it?"

"The Kent killing at the Starlight Estates, you working on it?"

"Along with about ten other killings."

"I thought I'd take you out to supper."

"A fancy place?"

"You pick it, Art."

"I haven't had anything but hamburger since the last time you bought me a steak. Maybe I'm in the wrong business. You working now, Hardman?"

"Steak then."

"And you're going to pick my mind?"

"If I can find it."

"I'll dust it off for you." He hesitated and shifted gears. "You knew him pretty well, didn't you? Kent or Ronny or whatever name he went by?"

"And liked him," I said.

We set up a meeting at Swain's Steak House. Later in the day I called and made a reservation for three.

The Starlight Estates is one of those "rip up the earth and tear down the trees" developments. A godawful waste: they knocked down a forest of fifty-year-old trees, cleared it and rolled it as flat as a table top, and then they put up rows and rows of apartments and condominiums. That done, they scooped out a hole and called it a lake. Finally they spent a small fortune planting truckloads of year-old trees. In about fifty years it might be a place where somebody might want to live.

Hump stayed in the car. I walked across a stubbly grass lawn to the resident manager's apartment. In the pocket of my jacket I had one of the last of the business cards that said I was an agent for Nationwide Insurance. It was finger-marked and one corner drooped like a hound's ear. Either I'd have to order some more or I'd have to think up another con. The last time I used it the old lady held the card at a distance, afraid, I guess, that she might catch some germs that were hidden around the raised lettering.

The man who answered the bell was about sixty, thin and spare and very much aware of his position. One look at him and I had to fight back a laugh. He wore a dark suit, a regimental tie and bedroom slippers. He wasn't wearing socks and I could see the puffy blue veins on his ankles.

I said good morning and handed him the card. He narrowed his eyes and peered at it. He shook his head sadly and got his glasses from the breast pocket of his suit coat. After he read the card, he handed it back to me. "I already have enough."

"It's not that. I'm here about Mr. Kent."

"John?"

"That's right." I was watching his face. He couldn't decide which way to go. His face was sad but there was also a trace of distaste there too. In the end, I think he told himself to smooth it away and let me guess.

"John was insured with you?"

"For years," I said.

He waved me into the apartment. It was neat, almost old-maidish. I didn't see any sign of a woman's touch. It was likely there wasn't one. I sat down on the sofa and reached for a cigarette before I saw the look on his face. He didn't approve and I dropped the pack back in my pocket.

"You'll still pay off... after the way John died?"

"Not if we can help it," I said.

He understood that. It was what most people believed about insurance companies anyway. Good touch there, Hardman. One gold star.

"His niece the beneficiary?"

I didn't know how to play that one. Might as well trip and fall on my nose. "Niece? I didn't know he had one."

"I thought so." He was smug, pleased with himself. His nose wrinkled, the way it does when you smell something bad but you don't want to admit you know what it is.

"His brother's the beneficiary. I don't know anything about a niece." Sometimes with these old ones you have to prime the pump more than once.

"That's what he said."

"What?"

"That she was his niece. And it was terrible, an old man like him carrying on with a girl who was thirty or forty years younger than he was."

Odd thing about upright people. The pictures they get in their heads are just as dirty as the ones in ours. And more often than not, they get the details in sharper focus. I grinned at him, the half leer that is the secret handshake of the traveling sales-man. "A pretty girl?"

"Pretty enough if you like that kind."

"Blonde?"

"Naw. Dark hair, black as coal dust."

"Built?"

"Not to my taste. If I was young, I'd have passed her up."

"Culled her," I said.

"That's right." The pump was running. He was warming up to it. "Kind of on the skinny side. Little teeny tits not much bigger than crabapples."

"A tall girl?"

"You know John?"

"Like I said, for years."

"She was about as tall as he was."

That would make her five-five or six. "He tell you her name?"

"He did more than that. Had the brass of a billy-goat. He introduced us."

"Remember her name?"

I guess I'd pushed too hard. He looked at me shrewdly. "You sure you're from that insurance company?"

"Nationwide," I said.

"You're asking a lot of strange questions."

"I have to. What if something happens to the brother before the estate is settled? If there's another relative I might need to know who she is."

"It won't be her," he said.

I got out a pad and uncapped my pen. I wanted it to look official.

"He called her Reggie. He said it was short for Regina."

"Last name?" I let him watch while I wrote down NIECE? REGINA (REGGIE).

"Don't remember it, but it wasn't Kent."

I added a big question mark and closed the pad. "She visit him often?"

"Weekends mainly. Now, that's what made me think…"

"How long did John live here?"

"The last year or so. Since the Estates opened."

"She visit him the whole year?"

"Just the last two or three months."

I capped the pen and jammed it back in my shirt pocket. "It was terrible what happened to him."

"You think it was terrible—you should have been with me when I found him."

"You did? I didn't know that."

He nodded. "You see, it was late Saturday afternoon. He didn't have a color TV set." He nodded toward a small Sony on a low table that faced the sofa. "There was a football game coming on from out on the west coast. You know how they start late. Well, I waited for him and when he didn't show up, I went down there to get him. He didn't come to the door when I knocked. I got worried. With people my age and his age… well, you have to worry. So I used my passkey and went in." He blinked at me. "Lord, I never saw anything like it and I hope I never do again. You know how much blood a person has in him? It looked like three or four times that much."

"They'd been rough on him?"

"Cut on him. Stripped the skin off him like you'd slice a piece off a side of bacon. And burned him. Burned his face and chest and his… privates."

"You must watch the place pretty close. You see anybody at his apartment the night before?"

"One person. It was like I told the police. I saw that niece of his with him. It was about seven that night."

"You see her leave?"

"Not that night. You see, Friday's my night for bingo at the Legion. That's how I know she was at the apartment. I went over to ask him if he wanted to go play bingo with me. As soon as he answered the door, I knew she was there."

"See her?"

"Not exactly, but I could smell her perfume and right past him I could see her coat where she'd dumped it over the back of a chair."

"Sure it was her?"

"It couldn't have been anybody else. Didn't any other woman visit him except her."

"And when you got back from bingo?"

"It was after midnight. His lights were out. I thought he'd gone to bed."

The pump was running down. I primed it again. "The girl's car still out front?"

"No." He closed his eyes. "In fact, I'm not even sure I saw her car that night. She drove this little car, a tan Pinto." He opened his eyes. "But that might not mean anything. Sometimes he'd drive in and pick her up. And other times, even when she drove out, she couldn't find a parking spot out in front of his apartment and had to park down the street a ways."

I stood up and held out my hand. "I appreciate you taking the time to talk to me, Mr ...?"

"Purvis," he said. "Ken Purvis."

He followed me to the door. "You don't remember the tag numbers on her Pinto, do you?"

"Police asked me the same thing." He shook his head. "It didn't mean much to me at the time and it really wasn't any of my business what John did and what girls he saw."

I got out to the porch before he stopped me. "One thing just came back to me. It was something I forgot and didn't tell the police. I think she was a dancer."

I turned and leaned into the doorway. I could smell the sourness of him on the warm air that rushed past him. "What makes you think that?"

"Something he said or something she said. I can't remember exactly."

I looked down the row of apartment entrances. "That might be helpful, Mr. Purvis."

"Hoped it might."

Might as well try it. "Which apartment was John's?"

"Third one down."

"Any chance of looking around?"

"Of course not." He seemed shocked that I'd asked.

"Huh?"

"Police orders," he said.

I waved at him. A good citizen accepting it when rebuffed. Another gold star on my book. Back at the car, Hump was huddled over, shivering. I drove back to town and found a restaurant where we could have lunch and a couple of drinks.

With a shot of J&B in me and lunch ordered, I carried my second drink over to the pay phone and called the Police Morgue. Somebody there said the body of John Kent had been released to the Callenwald Funeral Home. A secretary there said there would be no public viewing of the body because the brother had decided upon cremation. But there would be a memorial service the next morning at eleven at the Broadside Methodist church.

Art found us in the bar at Swain's. It was about five of seven. We carried our drinks into the dining room and Art ordered a beer. Art is moon-faced and so damned Irish-looking that you'd want to cast him in crowd scenes in any I.R.A. movie you were making. Or as the pub keeper. I've known him for almost twenty years, from the time we both were on the force. He was whippet-fast and quick then. He's slowed some and put on some weight, but not as much as I have.

He lowered the menu and looked at me. "I guess we're going to have to talk sooner or later."

"For your supper?" I grinned at him.

"I might have had to talk to you anyway."

"Why?"

"You knew Ronny pretty well. I didn't."

"This is a switch. I thought I was going to pick your mind."

"Let's call it a trade."

"I heard a few things in the last day or two. You might already know them."

"Try me," he said.

"Ronny was tapped-out and even worse he'd lost his gambler's nerve."

"Broke?"

"That's what I heard."

Art looked back down at the menu. "That would blow one theory all to hell."

"You check his bank?"

"A couple of thousand in savings. Two or three hundred in checking."

That would fit what The Man had told me. I dipped my head at Hump. "You want the prime rib?"

"About ten pounds of it," Hump said.

"You know as well as I do," Art continued, "that gamblers don't use banks any more than they have to."

"So you people think somebody went after his stash of play money?"

"It happens."

"The stash was gone. He'd lost it."

"I'd need to check that. Tell me where you heard it."

"It was passed in confidence," I said.

"You believe it?"

"Until I hear something that swings it the other way."

He made a crease down the menu with one fingernail. "You working, Jim, or is this some kind of private vendetta?"

"You know I can't work, Art. It'd be against the law. I'm not licensed by the Secretary of State."

"You could be," Art said.

"I've got better things to do with my money."

"Money?" Hump looked puzzled.

"To get licensed as a private detective, I'd have to post a ten thousand dollar bond. I'd have to pay a couple of hundred a year to keep the license. And there's a board that would have to decide if I was respectable enough to get the license in the first place. That kind of crap."

"You changing the subject on me, Jim?"

"Trying to." I laughed at him.

"Would you say you were doing a favor for somebody?" "Favor" is what I call it when I talk about being hired to do one of these odd jobs. "Maybe."

"Anybody I know?"

"I hope not. First thing you know you'll be trying to get into her pants too."

He didn't believe me. But he knew he couldn't push it. "Is it big enough for both of us?"

I nodded. "And the cab of one Mack truck."

"For this favor, what exactly are you doing?"

"I talked to the Resident Manager at the Starlight Estates."

"Sell him some insurance?"

"You find the girl yet?" I said to get back to him.

"It's harder than that. We found a brother out in Chamblee. He said he didn't know anything about a niece. As far as he knows, he's Ronny's only living relative."

"That Friday night, anybody in the other apartments hear anything?"

"Nothing. It happens that way sometimes. The apartment on the right is empty. The one on the left is rented to three stewardesses. All three were on flights that night."

"Looks like one of them could have managed to be on the rag," I said.

"Not anymore," Art said. "Not with the pill."

"Blanks and more blanks."

Art stopped worrying the menu. "The prime rib good here?"

"I don't know, but it's usually a good index for the rest of the food."

"I'll risk it."

The waitress must have had the table bugged. She hovered over us seconds later and I ordered prime rib for the three of us. After she left, I said, "That resident manager, Purvis, he came up with a bit he said he hadn't told the police. He can't place it exactly but he thinks the girl, Regina, is a dancer."

"That doesn't exactly open the door wide. You know how many dancers are working here in Atlanta?"

"Nobody said it was going to be easy."

Hump rattled the ice cubes in his empty glass. He listens good and I find myself wondering what he thinks about the crap Art and I talk about when we get together. "How'd he die, Art?"

"You know him, Hump?"

"Saw him a time or two."

"According to the M.E., his heart gave out on him."

"Rough?"

"The apartment smelled like the cook got drunk and burned the roast. You ever handle a soldering iron?"

"Never by the wrong end," Hump said.

"Somebody used the wrong end on him. They did everything but write the Lord's Prayer on him. His balls looked like somebody'd cooked them on a barbecue grill."

"Mean shit." Hump turned and looked at me. I had the feeling he knew I wanted to ask but couldn't bring myself to it. I'd guessed it hadn't been pretty, and I wanted to walk around it if I could.

The bottom fell out of the talk. We sipped fresh drinks and waited for the prime rib.

After supper, we walked out to the car with Art. It was cold and moist, a bad wet cold. Art unlocked his car and opened the door and turned and leaned on it. "I'll try the angle that the girl is a dancer. All the girls who work in clubs have to be licensed by the city."

"Better if we had a last name."

"That would be too easy. If it was that easy, I'd solve my ten murders in the next two hours and go on vacation." He blew his fog breath at me. "Way down south where the sun is."

"There's a memorial service for Ronny in the morning. I thought I'd look in at it."

"You think that girl Reggie or Regina is going to be that dumb?"

"Maybe. I knew this woman once." I'd started to say spade woman and stopped myself. "Her husband died in the hospital. Doctors had it down as a natural death. Some young intern asks her if they can do an autopsy. Dumb broad gives her permission. They find enough poison in him to wipe out Tucker, Georgia. We start checking back and find she'd collected insurance on two other husbands. Dug them up and found poison in them, too. Last I heard, she was still doing time."

"That girl didn't know what *autopsy* meant. I'll bet she thought it was a new way of combing a dead man's hair." He turned, bent over and got into the car. "You'll be at the service?" I nodded. "No reason for me to stop by then."

I stepped back and he closed the door.

The Man came on the line a few seconds after I gave my name to the soldier who'd answered the phone.

"Yeah, Hardman?"

"Any calls?"

"Nothing."

"I guess they're still counting last night's take."

He didn't say anything.

"You know anything about Ronny's personal life the last two or three months?"

"A man his age?"

"He ever mention a girl named Regina?"

"Not to me."

"Any of the old crowd stay close to him the last year or two?"

"Most of them are dead," The Man said. "Maybe Mort Heppler did."

"I'd like to talk to him."

Hump came in from the kitchen. He put a scotch and water on the night table and went into the living room.

"The way he is most of the time, you couldn't get within fifty feet of him without a roof falling on you. Let me try to reach him. I'll call you back."

"I'm at home."

He hung up and I carried my drink into the living room. Hump had the TV tuned to channel 17. He'd found a Hawks game. It was the same old crap. The Hawks were playing like they already knew the season was over and they'd already packed for their end of the season vacation.

"You free right now?" The Man asked when he called back.

"Sure."

"You know the Dogwood Lounge?"

I did. I'd passed it a number of times but I'd never gone in. It was pretty far out Peachtree Road. It was on the ground level of one of those huge apartment towers. I'd heard it was expensive and that it had a reputation as a pick-up place. Widows and divorcees with a little money did their drinking there. I guess they figured if you were a guy who could afford the tab, your social position was high enough to rate a try at picking them up.

"Mort owns it. He says to tell the doorman you're expected."

"Thanks."

"Get on with it," he said. "You drag your feet and I can expect another money phone call."

He chopped the line. I stopped off at my closet and took out my tie rack. I carried it into the living room with me. It was halftime and Skip Carey, in that bland pudding manner of his that passed for humor, was interviewing some expert or other from the other team.

"Pick one."

"We got an invitation to a rich place?"

"Not exactly."

Hump fingered two or three of the ties. "Shit, I'm going to have to leave a few of mine over here. These look like you got them from a rag picker."

I gave him his choice. He didn't like any of them.

The doorman in front of the Lounge eased himself around on the balls of his feet and stared at us. He was looking, I thought, for an excuse not to let us in. Drunk already or not wearing a tie, maybe even mud on our shoes. From the long time he kept his eyes on Hump I was certain there weren't many blacks who didn't get turned away for one reason or another.

"You want something?"

"Heppler's expecting us."

He couldn't take his eyes of Hump. Maybe he'd never seen a black that big before. "You're Hardman?" I nodded. "I didn't hear anything about two of you."

"My uncle goes everywhere I do."

His face twisted at that, the wrinkles chewing on it, and when he couldn't come up with what he thought was a suitable volley, he turned and led us into the Lounge, past a coat room where a slat-thin girl in a pink wig motioned that she'd take our coats. We didn't stop, followed the doorman over thick dark carpeting and down a low flight of stairs into a basin-like room. A big room. Careful and low lighting. Hardly a shadow would perch on a wrinkle down there. In the center of the room, there was a huge circular bar with a piano built into one end of it. It was early or the piano player was on a break. He was dark, Cuban-looking, with a cigarette wet-lipped in the corner of his mouth, his hands doing idle tinkling. The tune wasn't anything I could whistle.

About eight or nine women at the bar. A couple of them butterflying around the piano player. At the small tables spaced around the bar, the usual pairs of women. Never out to drink alone. That was America for you. The women dressed with the smell of money on them. As we marched through behind the doorman, the casual look around at us that had the right degree of boredom in it, but underneath the hungry that nothing could kick sand over.

"Back here." We'd reached a door with PRIVATE in script on it.

Down a narrow hallway. Another door at the end. Nothing written on this door. He waved us to a stop and tapped on the door and stepped back. A minute later, a young tough opened the door. A screw-you in the pale blue eyes that looked past the doorman at Hump and me. Curly straw-colored hair that he was trying to straighten. He wore a dark plaid suit with the waist pinched and the cuffs flared. It was two-eighty off the rack and a few days to get the fit just right at the tailor's.

"Mr. Heppler's expecting them," the doorman said.

"You're Hardman then?"

I just looked at him. I didn't nod or smile or wink.

"Who's he?" He dipped his head at Hump.

"With me. He's my partner."

"Nothing said about him."

"We going to stand out in the hallway all night?"

I started past him. He put up a hand, hard against my chest. The doorman stepped around behind me and ran his hands down me. When the doorman grunted and moved away from me, I looked over my shoulder at him. He'd approached Hump. Hump turned slowly and looked at him.

"I'm not carrying."

"I've got to check you," the doorman said.

"Do your fag tricks somewhere else." Hump opened his coat and showed them there wasn't anything in his waistband.

The doorman angled a look at the stud in the doorway. He got his instructions and backed away.

"I'm Tony Mitchell," the guy in the doorway said. He backed against the doorframe to let us pass. I could smell sandalwood on him, so much of it that he wore it like a loose coat. We were in a reception room. There was a closed door straight ahead and he led us in that direction. When he reached the door, he didn't knock. He gripped the knob and turned back to us. "I didn't get your name," he said to Hump.

Hump gave him a smile with all the good will scraped off it. "Fuck you, Charlie."

It registered on Mitchell and he gave it some consideration. He might have done something about it if the man inside hadn't said, "Are you coming in or not?"

The man behind the desk didn't get up. I'm not sure he could have. He looked about seventy. What we used to call TB-thin and tall, about six-four or five. His skin had the pallor of death before the undertaker brushes the rouge on. The alive part of him was his hands. Without seeming to know what they were doing, like they weren't a part of him, he was playing with a deck of cards. From the moves, he was a damned good mechanic.

"This is Mr. Hardman and his partner didn't give his name." Mitchell remained at the doorway behind us.

"For good reason," I said. "The frisk was cheap shit. We came here with good words on us."

I watched his hands. He was dealing seconds, doing it slowly at first, and then after I was sure what he was up to, speeding it so that I lost him. "A frisk, Tony?"

"There wasn't anything said about a second man, Mr. Heppler. I thought that was reason enough."

"Find anything on us?" I asked it without looking around at him.

"No."

"That's all, Tony," Heppler said.

The door closed behind us. I waited a beat or two before I looked over my shoulder. He'd gone into the reception room.

"He's something of a hot-head," Heppler said.

"So am I," I said.

Heppler sized Hump up. "Maybe you could introduce me to your partner."

"Hump Evans," I said.

"I've heard about you." Heppler scooped up the cards, tapped them on the desk and put them aside. "Our mutual friend said you're looking into what happened to Ronny."

"That's right."

"Have a chair." He waited until we were seated. "You know Ronny long?"

"Twenty years off and on."

"Play cards with him?"

"A few times."

"Win much?"

I laughed. "Not as much as I lost."

"In his time, he had it all. Nerves, the instincts, and a head like a machine."

"I heard he lost it."

"He did. Lost his nerve. After that the rest of it wasn't worth two sheets of shit paper."

"How?"

"He used to go to Vegas a few times a year. One time, a couple of years ago, he got into a big game. The way I heard it from out there, he ran into a man who had better cards. Ronny's instincts said one thing and his head said another. He trusted his instincts and got his guts ripped out and spread on the card table."

"Bad," I said.

"It happens. It's the business risk."

"You see much of him the last few months, Mr. Heppler?"

"One night every week. Usually Wednesdays. A low stakes game between friends."

"He win?"

"Food and beer money," Heppler said. "That is, when he had the cards."

There'd been a beat, a breath too much in there. I read it the other way. They'd been friends for a long time. A friend couldn't offer a tapped-out man cash unless he asked for it. But a friend could play a few stupid hands of cards once a week. "Ronny didn't see through it?"

"See through what?"

I let it drop. "He talk to you much about his personal life?"

"That would have been a ten-second conversation. You know he never got married? Well, he liked women, but he liked cards more. His good years he had a way with the girls."

"He didn't talk to you about a girl he was spending time with the last two or three months?"

"No." He smiled a tired smile. "If there was one, I'm happy for him. And grateful to the girl."

"How'd he spend his time? He tell you?"

"Only what he wanted to. And it wasn't much."

That matched what I knew of him. He was friendly but he didn't talk a lot about himself. It was like that was a part of him that wasn't any of your business.

"I've run out of questions. Except for one."

"Which question is that?" He lifted the cards and began to toy with them.

"Who killed him?"

"If I knew that, I'd tell you where to find the body."

The reception room was empty. So Mitchell hadn't waited around to kiss us good-by after all. His kiss would have left a hickey anyway.

Hump said, "That didn't tell us much."

"A couple of things. Now we know what he did on Wednesdays and we know he didn't talk about the girl, Regina, even to his best friends."

"The first part of that scares me," Hump said.

"Huh?"

"It means we're going to have to find out what he did the other six days of the week? Is it that long a job?"

"Now you've got it."

Out in the Lounge the Cuban-looking piano player had drawn a few more butterflies. It was flutter-flutter, snap your fingers, while he played "Green Dolphin Street."

We stepped out into the windy cold. The doorman wasn't in sight. I stopped and looked in both directions. "You think Heppler might have been telling us something?"

"About Mitchell being a hot-head?"

"Maybe."

"Fuck him," Hump said.

We rounded the corner of the building and stepped off the walk onto the asphalt parking lot. My car was away from the building, to the right near a border of young trees. It was dark there, and we were a few feet away, when the doorman eased into the light. He'd been waiting in the tree border.

"You stealing hubcaps?" I said.

He let that slide off him. He opened his jacket so that I could see the butt of his iron. Footsteps behind us now that we were fronted. I turned and looked. It was Tony Mitchell. I guessed he'd been waiting against the side of the building.

"You people got a script for this?" I said.

The doorman said, "Tony doesn't like spades with big mouths."

"But both of you love me?"

"You and me," the doorman said, "we don't have to dance unless you really want to."

"That's what the iron's for? So I won't ask you to dance?"

"I don't need the piece." But the doorman didn't make a move to take the iron out and put it aside.

Hump took off his coat and handed it to me. "All this asshole wants is his introduction to me. Let it go at that."

"You sure?"

"I'm sure." He shucked off the tie. As he passed it to me, he said, in a whisper, "Keep the other one off my back."

"If you say so." I walked toward the doorman. He backed away until he was in the space between two cars, mine and a dark blue Mustang. His hand touched the butt of the piece.

"Relax," I said. "He wants me out of it."

"We watch?"

"That's it." He kept his distance. I wasn't as close as I wanted to be. I'd have to wait until the fight started, until he got distracted.

"Come on, cunt," Hump said, "tell me where you get your hair curled." He had his hands up and ready.

At first it was a dance, Mitchell circling him, his shoes making the scuff-scuff and his left flicking out, not coming within inches of Hump. And Mitchell was doing the snort-snort that was supposed to tell us that he'd trained some for the ring.

Hump watched him. He wasn't dancing. He was turning slowly, keeping Tony in front of him. "This one of those new dances where you don't touch?" Hump said.

Mitchell moved in. He was a lot faster than I'd thought. He used the left jab and Hump brushed that aside with a forearm. He hardly saw the right that hit him about cheek high. It rocked him some. It was a good punch and it was the first time I'd seen Hump hit that hard.

Mitchell rasped at him, "That better?"

The doorman was about to pee in his pants he was so happy. I took a step toward him. He didn't even notice. "Cut him up, Tony."

Another step. I was at arm length.

Hump hadn't thrown a punch. It wasn't his style against a boxer anyway. He wanted to get in close where he could use his strength. The way Mitchell could use that right, he'd have to take some punishment to get past it.

Slap. Slap. Mitchell used the left on him. Jabbing at him. About one in three got past the forearm. The lefts didn't have the steam of the right but they were bruising. In the long run, handling it that way, Mitchell could damage an eye or cut Hump's face up into little strips. It was a good thing Mitchell didn't have the patience. The success he'd had with the one right he'd thrown spoiled him. He wanted to use it again. Hump must have seen it the way I did. He waited him out.

When it came it ,was a good solid right. It hit Hump in the throat, but he'd taken most of the steam by ducking his head under his shoulder. Now, instead of dancing away, putting distance between them, he stepped in to Mitchell. He took one more right in the chest getting there. But he had Mitchell by the back of the neck and his left hand had Mitchell's right arm, pushing it out and away. This didn't stop Mitchell. He kept ramming his left into Hump's kidney. I could almost feel that left. From the way Hump jerked after each blow I knew they were hurting him.

The hand was behind Mitchell's head for a reason. Hump took the bad punishment while he steadied Mitchell's head. He leaned forward and butted Mitchell across the bridge of the nose. The crunch of Mitchell's nose getting spread across his face buried itself in the grunt that came out of Mitchell's mouth. The left quit digging into Hump's kidney. Hump released Mitchell's neck and grabbed the right arm high, about at the elbow. He turned and put a hip check on him and threw him. They were about twenty or thirty feet from the nearest car. Mitchell started out high but by the time he reached the car the arc had flattened out. He hit the car about bumper high. He grabbed at the bumper and tried to pull himself up. Hump didn't give him the time. He crossed the twenty or thirty feet in about three steps. His left pushed at Mitchell, straightening him up. He hit Mitchell about belly high with the right. The breath went out of him, part grunt and part fart.

Next to me the doorman started his move. He was level with me when his hand reached into his waistband and grabbed the butt of the iron. He thought I was giving way, making room. Instead I swung an elbow at him and caught him across the throat. He fell away and I jumped at him. My left hand grabbed him at the throat and bent him back over the tail end of the Mustang. My right hand pushed at the gun hand, shoving it downward so he could free it from his waistband.

"Turn it loose," I said. "It goes off and you'll need a new set of balls."

He kicked at me. I moved my leg and felt the rough edge of the shoe scrape the calf. I put more pressure on his throat. I heard another blow Hump threw into Mitchell. Mitchell didn't even grunt with this one. I didn't have time to look around. Footsteps and hard breathing behind me. Hump leaned across me.

"Get it," I said.

"Get what?"

"The gun hand—"

Hump caught the doorman by the bicep of his gun arm and squeezed. Just a few seconds and the arm went slack and dead. Hump pushed the arm aside. I reached in and grabbed the butt of the iron and jerked it out. I turned and threw it over the border of trees.

Hump leaned away. "Move him," he said to the doorman.

I let him pass. The doorman walked over and stood staring down at Mitchell. He was sprawled out on his face right behind my car. He didn't even twitch.

"Move him," Hump said, "or I'll back right over him."

The doorman squatted and caught Mitchell under the arms. He turned him and then, straightening up, dragged him a few feet to the side.

❧ ❧ ❧

At a stop light a few blocks away, after I'd caught a red, I shifted around in my seat and had my look at the damage. His right eye was puffed and there was a thin line of blood dripping out of the cut on the left corner of his mouth. I dug out a handkerchief and passed it to him and he pressed it against the cut.

"That was a waste of time," I said.

"Did seem silly, didn't it?"

"You think that was what it had written on the face of it? All that for some hurt feelings?"

He nodded. He'd taken the handkerchief to answer me and the shake of his head splattered some blood down across his shirt front. "Muscle has to prove itself now and then. In fact, he had to prove it to Heppler. Heppler might have expected it."

I dropped him in front of his apartment house and told him to sleep late the next morning. I'd be at the memorial service for Ronny.

He waved and got out and walked up the steps on shaky legs.

I waited until I saw him unlock the door and go inside before I started the long drive home.

All the way home I was bothered by the fight. It didn't make any sense. At the same time telling myself that out there among the meat-eaters, reason didn't have a lot to do with anything anyway.

CHAPTER FOUR

t was a strange ceremony. There were hothouse flowers on both sides of the pulpit and the minister, a young man who might have been a student chaplain, talked about Ronny as if he didn't know him. Of course, by mistake, he said some of the right things. It might have come out of some form sheet that the minister was handed in Bible college. All there but you had to fill in the dead man's name now and then. He talked about fairness and honesty and how John Kent had been a good man and the world was going to be the poorer because of his passing. Ronny ended up sounding like a Rotarian, a member of the Chamber of Commerce and a high ranking dues payer from the Fraternal Order of Elks.

I arrived early. There was an usher and he wanted to seat me down front. I shook him off and took the rear, left corner of the back pew. It was close enough to hear as much of the service as I wanted to and I had a good seat where I could study the arrivals and tag them as they entered.

The brother was easy. He was wearing a dark gray suit with an armband attached to the sleeve. He looked a little like Ronny and he even carried himself like him, a walk that was a cross between a jerk and a strut.

Mort Heppler came in a few minutes before the ceremony started. He was flanked by a new hard ass. When Mort saw me, he nodded once, very slowly, so that it seemed to take about a minute for the head to go down and bob back up. I couldn't read anything in his face. And I did want to know how he felt about the job Hump had done on his bodyguard. I made a note to call

The Man later and find out. It wouldn't do to cross Heppler's path again until I was sure he'd accepted the bad beating as something that Mitchell had asked for.

And the others came. I didn't know them by name. There was the blind ex-boxer, a black who'd been good back in the early 1940's, who could be seen any day selling brooms and brushes down on Five Points. I'd heard Ronny'd helped him now and then. And there was the big blonde waitress who worked in the coffee shop where Ronny'd eaten breakfast or lunch when he was downtown. The rumor was that Ronny liked to play Santa Claus for her two little girls.

The rest were the hustlers and the corner people. Wearing their best even if it was a little colorful. Uncomfortable in the church. I watched some of them during the service. They didn't know when to stand up or when to sit down. And no matter how bravely they sang, and no matter what the hymn was, it sounded like they were whistling "Stardust."

I got too involved. I was carrying on an under the breath dialogue with the young minister. I wasn't arguing with him, just correcting him when he slipped over the edge and made Ronny sound pure enough to run a Boy Scout troop. At the same time, I watched those sad old friends. There were some tears and the big blonde waitress gulped and sighed for her breath. Once, by craning my neck, I saw Mort Heppler rubbing at his nose like it itched.

A short prayer and it was over. By my watch, it had been twenty-five minutes. Like the hustlers and corner people, I hadn't known what to expect either.

I stood up. I decided it might be a good time to have a word with Heppler and find out how he felt about the fight the night before. When he was moved, touched, might be the best time. The outside aisle was empty. I went down it about halfway and cut across a pew, heading for the center aisle. I reached that aisle and found myself waiting for a slot in the traffic when I looked back toward the entranceway.

A girl was there. I had no way of knowing how long she'd been at the church. Dark-haired, small and pretty. And she didn't fit. Not with the other hustlers. I made my guess she was probably the Reggie or Regina we'd been looking for.

I made my own slot in the traffic and plowed toward the entranceway. I didn't get far. I had the bad luck to brush up against a big bruiser who must have been a bouncer at one time or another. He whirled on me and gave me a shocked look.

I said, "Excuse me," and tried to edge past him.

He caught my shoulder and the strength of that one hand numbed my arm right down to the tips of my fingers. "Mister, you show some respect for the dead."

"I've got to see somebody."

"Respect," he said. And he held my shoulder until I nodded. He released me then and I passed him at a slow walk. It took me a couple of minutes to reach the entranceway. The girl wasn't there anymore. I hurried out to the church steps and stood there, looking in both directions. Nothing. I remained there for another ten minutes, tagging each person and the car they got into, just in case she'd reached a car and hadn't driven off yet. It didn't work. She'd vanished. And I made the mistake of staying too long. The young minister came out and saw me and thought I'd stayed behind to talk to him. I had to shake his hand and say I liked what he had said about John Kent.

He was grave and modest and he wanted to comfort me in my time of grief. I lied and said I was comforted, very much so, and then I backed down the steps and got away before he made a reach for my soul. I could see he was leaning in that direction.

The eye wasn't as bad as I'd expected it to be. The cut on his lip was scabbing and there was a swelling on his left cheek where Hump had taken his best shot.

I unloaded the Care package I brought with me. Two half quart cartons of coffee and a dozen sausage biscuits wrapped in foil bags. I ate a couple of the sausage biscuits and drank my coffee while Hump stood under the shower for about twenty minutes.

Dressed and seated across from me, Hump took one bite from one of the biscuits and made a face. "You should have brought a milkshake."

"Jaw?"

"I think that bastard loosened a tooth or two on one side."

"Chew on the other side."

"You try that lately?"

I shook my head. "And I run away from fights too."

"Teach me how." He got up and opened the refrigerator and got a bottle of catsup. He poured a glop on each pattie and went on eating.

"The girl showed up."

"Regina or whatever?"

"I think so."

"Nice?"

"Prime trim you'd call her."

He swallowed and washed it down with a gulp of coffee. "You have a long talk with her?"

"Lost her in the crowd."

He laughed, spraying biscuit crumbs across the table at me.

"You up to working, Hump?"

"Finding that girl? Sure."

"I thought I had your interest," I said.

He went on eating.

"It ought to be easier now. I know what she looks like."

Freddie Glass likes to call himself the Nightclub Editor for the *Constitution*. He isn't but I've seen the byline slip through that way once or twice. They really hired him to do the usual scut work, the fires and bank robberies. About a year ago, with the usual sense that papers show, they transferred him to Amusements. He's been reviewing movies and plays since and he doesn't know anything about plays and even less about film. He works under the Amusement Editor who used to write sports. So much for the level of criticism in Atlanta.

What Freddie really wants to do is set up a separate desk for the nightclub beat. He's been making that pitch for half a year. He has this dream of having a special table set aside for him at all the clubs and they'll furnish him free drinks and free food and he'll have so much power the young girls will drop their drawers for him to get their names in the paper.

That is, Freddie is horny and on the make.

A girl at the desk said Freddie was out on assignment and, when I pushed, she said he was at the Dream Gate South, a club on West Peachtree near Ponce de Leon. It seemed early in the day for nightclubbing but I wanted to see him. We drove down and parked in the crowded lot next door to the club.

The banner above the club entrance had red letters about six inches high. MISS NAKED WORLD APPEARING NOW. Hand on the door I could hear a drum roll from inside. We went in.

A young guy in a white Gatsby suit met us one step inside the door. "Which paper?"

"*Northside News*," I said.

Hump said, "*Black World*."

The young guy seemed to have heard of both of them. He waved a hand at the bar. "Drinks and food. Help yourself."

We drifted in the direction of the bar. Trays of drinks were made up. I sniffed at some of them until I found some watered-down scotch. I passed one to Hump and got another for me.

The club was full. I could see a few newspaper men I knew. Some of them were from sports and others from the police beat. It looked like the free drinks and food had brought them all out.

I located Freddie at a table down front. That was like him. Get there early and find the best spot. Chubby, thick glasses gleaming, the pasty look of a choir boy who'd taken up drink.

Up on the stage, dressed in a red suit with gold lapels, a short barrel of a man was saying, "... guess you're wondering why I asked you here, why I spent two thousand alone on the catering."

A couple of people at a table over to the right laughed.

"Would you believe two dollars and ninety-eight cents?"

More laughter.

"Well, here she is. Miss Naked World."

There was another drum roll and a red-haired girl came out on the stage. She was barefooted and wearing a dark green kimono robe. Even before she reached the chair in the center of the stage, she unbelted the robe and opened it wide. She wasn't wearing a stitch under it. She peeled it from her shoulders and passed it to the man in the red suit.

"I feel more comfortable this way," she said. "I hate clothes."

The face wasn't much. The rest of her was. The only thing that bothered me a bit was the color of her pubic hair. It was the same shade of showgirl red that her wig was. In fact, it might have been a wig too.

I edged over and found the food. There were some dips and crackers, a pan of meatballs and some chicken livers wrapped in bacon. I did some eating while the question and answer session got underway.

Between stabs at the food, I watched Freddie Glass. He was staring at her crotch and asking her a question. I could see the oil sweat on his forehead.

Hump and I waited out on the walk for Freddie. He was one of the last to leave. I guess he couldn't get enough of that pink muff and he'd brought up a last question or two to give him a reason to stay behind.

"You here, Jim?" he asked.

"Needed a word with you."

We'd started away when a heavy man in the red suit with the gold lapels came to the door and shouted, "Now you write a good story, you hear?"

Freddie waved at him. "What's it about?"

I described the girl I'd seen in the doorway of the church. I told him I thought she might be a dancer.

"I haven't seen her," Freddie said. "Maybe she works in a top-less place. Not my beat."

"I don't think so." I remembered the way she looked. Too much class for those places.

He unlocked his Buick and tossed his note pad on the seat. "I'll ask around. Regina's the name?"

"That's right."

"I'll call you if I hear anything."

I patted his shoulder as he got into the Buick. He drove away to write his story. Visions of pink muffs dancing behind his eyelids.

Later that afternoon, I dropped Hump at his place and drove back to the Starlight Estates. I parked in a slot in front of the resident manager's apartment and tried the doorbell. No answer. I walked down to the apartment Purvis had pointed out as belonging to Ronny.

I tried the door. It was unlocked. I pushed it and went in. There were packing cases all around the living room.

"Anybody here?"

Ronny's brother came to the bedroom doorway. He was still wearing the suit with the black armband. "You want something here?"

It wasn't unfriendly, just irritated. I'd interrupted him in his work.

"I knew Ronny for a long time."

He stared at me for a moment. "I think I saw you at the service."

"I was there." I stepped around a couple of packing cases and held out my hand. I gave him my name and he told me he was Joe Bob Kent. He had a wary, puzzled look and I was fairly certain he wasn't the right one to use the insurance agent gambit with. So I told the truth.

He heard me out. At the end he said, "But you're not a policeman?"

"Not anymore."

"Then how can you investigate—?"

"Easier than you think."

"I'm not sure I ought to trust you."

"You talk to somebody at the police?"

"A Mr. Mahoney."

"It's Maloney," I said. I nodded at the phone next to the sofa. "It still connected?"

"I think so."

I went over and dialed Art's home number. Edna answered and after I got past some small talk I got Art on the line. I turned the phone over to Joe Bob Kent and walked into the bedroom. Now it seemed bare and spartan. The mattress where the butchery had been done was gone and through the springs. I could see some dark stains on the floor that I knew were blood. So I looked at the walls. I could see the stick-on hooks and the dust outlines where the pictures had been. On the cleared dresser top there were stacks of pictures, some framed and some not. Off to one side about a foot of old newspapers. I'd interrupted Joe Bob while he was wrapping the pictures and packing them away.

While I waited for him to end his talk with Art, I looked through the stack of old photos. Some of the larger frames held four and five pictures. The old ones were black and white, now browning with age. Ronny had been young then. Most were taken in nightclubs or by a pool. The other men in the photos were like Ronny had been then, the high roller types. In some there were girls, the showgirl types, the ones you could buy for a night with a few leftover chips.

At the bottom there were the more recent ones. They were color and they were in the folders that they came in. Linen-like paper with the beauty shot photo of the hotel or club on front. I'd culled through most of these before I realized that Joe Bob was in the doorway, watching me.

"He says you're a mustang, but you're honest up to a point."

"That's a fair estimate," I said.

I opened another of the folders as I talked. It froze me, the picture there. It was a recent picture of Ronny. He was at a nightclub. The dazzle of a white tablecloth. Ronny wearing a dark suit. The girl next to him, without the showgirl smile, with the serious look of someone who didn't want her picture taken, was the girl I'd seen in the entranceway to the church. I looked at the cover of the folder. The Sands Hotel.

I carried the picture over to Joe Bob. "You know this girl?"

He hardly looked at it. "I didn't know any of his women."

"Women" sounded like whore, the way he said it.

"She was at the service this morning," I said.

"Was she?" He peered down at the picture. "I didn't see her."

"You mind if I keep this for a day or two? I'll have copies made and mail it back to you."

"I guess it's all right." He got out a shoulder wallet and gave me his card. It said that he was a real estate dealer and gave both his office and his home address.

I put that in my pocket and closed the photo folder. I looked around. "You find anything odd here?"

"Everything about John was odd."

I felt the strong disapproval. He'd done his duty by his brother and that had included a memorial service. Now the truth was slipping out. He'd never understood Ronny and he never would.

"He was a good man," I said.

He accepted it as another of those nice lies you tell the family about the black sheep. The ones the family chewed up and spat out later. It saddened me some, the gap between what Ronny had been and the way his brother saw him.

I thanked him and left him standing next to the dresser, staring down at the photographic proof of the kind of life Ronny had led. The bad life, the wasted life.

I drove to the photo lab on Piedmont. As soon as I decided to have some copies made I thought of Jimmy. I'd helped him get a job five years ago when he'd come up for parole. I think that carried some weight with the Board: the man who'd put the collar on him thinking he was worth paroling.

It was a lab that processed a lot of the film that came in from the little drugstores all over the city. It wasn't an impressive building, just a cinderblock cube with one window up front and a couple of van trucks parked out there with "Quickie Film Processing" on the sides.

The girl in the office called for him and I leaned on the counter and waited. Jimmy came through the doorway like he didn't have a worry in the world. A black in his late twenties, mod dresser. A scar that ran down from his right ear. He'd gotten that in the slam when he fought off a big stud who wanted to punk him.

He saw me and his feet got stuck in mud, but he came in. He leaned across the counter, his voice a low and intense whisper. "I'm clean, Hardman, and you know it."

I grinned at him. "You must be clean. Otherwise you'd know I'm not a cop anymore."

"Really?" He straightened up. "In that case, what can I do for you, Mr. Hardman?"

I opened the folder and took the photo out of the brackets. "I need a dozen copies of this. A rush job. After you've made the copies, slice them. I just want the girl's picture."

"It'll cost you."

"Twenty?"

"You going to wait?"

"I'll wait."

I sat on a bench and smoked a cigarette or two. Passing the time I turned the folder and read the back. I hadn't noticed it before. It gave the name and address of the photo lab in Vegas. The Willow Co. Below that: For additional copies, send $4.98 and the date this picture was taken along with this photo. Lots of luck there. And then as I turned the folder, I saw a faint impression below this come-on. It was just deep enough for me to read. 11/23/72. From the smudge I could guess that Ronny had made the notation so he'd remember that in case he wanted another print. And later he'd erased that pencil mark.

It was half an hour by the clock when Jimmy returned with the copies. I put the original photo back in the folder and slipped him the twenty. He smooth-handed it off the counter and into his pocket. I took the dozen trimmed-down copies.

"Stay clean, Jimmy."

He met my eyes. "I've got a wife and a boy now. That sound like somebody wants to do hard time?"

I agreed with him that it didn't.

From a pay booth down the road I called Hump's apartment. He answered on the second ring. "Glad you called, Jim. The Man wants to see you."

"He say what it was about?"

"Said he had a tape he wants you to hear."

Shit. The second demand. I'd been expecting it, but not this soon. I wasn't close enough. I was following the string but I couldn't see the end of it.

"I'll meet you there."

"Twenty minutes," Hump said.

"I tried to stall them for a day or two," The Man said.

"Try for a week."

I opened the folder and passed the picture to him. The Man turned so that the light came from over his shoulder. "This the girl?"

"I need to talk to her and she's in town."

He looked at the beauty shot on the folder cover. "Sands, huh?"

I turned the folder so that he could see the faint impression. "See it? The date?"

The Man nodded.

"You have contacts out there?"

"Some." He flipped back to the photo. "Seems a bit young for old Ronny."

"Spread some bread on the Vegas waters. Describe the photo to them. Have them trace down a copy. Have them walk the photo around the places where Ronny did his play. Somebody might know her."

"All club girls look alike."

"Look at her again. She's not the type. I doubt she was selling it for chips."

He closed the folder. I got out the business card Joe Bob Kent had given me. "After you make the call, have one of your boys mail the photo to this address."

"All right. Here's the call." He reached out and punched the "Play" button.

"*You were a twenty short,*" the mushmouth man said.

"*It was a rush,*" The Man said. "*Mistakes happen.*"

"*Bad faith bothers me. I think we're going to have to renegotiate.*"

"*What does that mean?*"

"Good acting there," I said to The Man.

"*You saw the xerox copies of the two pages?*"

"*I saw them,*" The Man said. "*And you talk to me about good and bad faith.*"

A laugh that fluttered on the tape. "*The price just went up. For these copies the price is a hundred thousand.*"

"*That's steep. How do I know you didn't make a dozen copies of each page?*"

"*You don't. You'll have to trust me.*"

"*I did before. It didn't work.*"

Hump said, "Just the right amount of outrage."

"*Make the same arrangements. The fat man, Hardman, to make the drop again.*"

"*It'll take time to get that much money together,*" The Man said. "*And there's another problem.*"

"*Huh?*"

"*I don't think Hardman will do it.*"

"Good thinking there," I said.

"*Jack the money up. He'll sell strips of his ass for a hundred-dollar bill.*"

"*He says he's out of it,*" The Man said.

"*Jesus Christ, that's your problem. You convince him.*"

"*It'll take time.*"

"*I'll call back in two days.*"

The Man hit the "Stop" button before the line went dead. Hump got up and headed for the bar. He was grinning when he passed me. "It sounds like he knows you well, Jim."

"That remark about selling strips of my ass? I didn't know I was a town character."

The Man lifted the receiver and began dialing. "Fix yourself a drink while I call Vegas."

I played barman while Hump sat on the sofa and stretched his long legs. "That bother you?"

I dropped a couple of cubes in two glasses and splashed on J&B. "What?"

"That he insists on you making the drop. Nobody else."

I carried him his drink. "Maybe he heard around town that I was incompetent."

"Maybe, or maybe he's somebody you know or you knew."

"Someone who doesn't like me."

"And the way he talks."

"Yeah?" I sipped at the scotch and waited. Hump didn't talk a lot most of the time, a lot of funny crap mostly, but when he got an idea it usually had some shine to it.

"What do you think it is?"

I said, "Something in his mouth, chewing gum."

"Reminds me something happened to me." He tapped his glass on the coffee table. "Knew this prime trim once. Name was Ethel. Didn't know it at the time ,but she had false teeth. Walked in on her one morning." He grinned. "I was going to wake her up with my special early morning perk-me-up. Found her snoring away without her teeth." He waved a hand toward the kitchen-dining room where the tape recorder was. "Talked like that man while she was running me out of her bedroom."

"Mad with you?"

"Some. Got over it after she had her teeth in and we were taking this hot and friendly shower together."

"Let me see if I've got this profile. He's a stud who knows and doesn't like me and he's wearing false teeth, except when he's making phone calls to The Man."

He knew it was weak. He shrugged. "Good way to disguise your voice."

"Why?"

"Why what?"

"Why go to the trouble?"

"Must be some reason," Hump said.

"A couple of things. He doesn't know about the tape recorder. No way he could guess I'd hear his voice during the calls. One possibility is that The Man knows him and might recognize his voice. Two: I heard his voice over at the Omni. It didn't even sound familiar. So this crap where he acts like he knows so much about me. It's just to send us down some wrong alleys."

The Man came up from the kitchen-dining room and leaned against the bar. "I talked to a security man at the hotel I stay at when I'm out there. He knew Ronny. He'll start on it right now and he might have something for us by morning."

"Call me soon as you hear anything." I stood up and stretched and tossed down the J&B. "I'm bushed and it's still early."

"You're staking a lot on finding the girl. What if it doesn't work out?"

"Then I've made a bad guess and the police have too."

Hard eyes sliced at me. "And it'll cost me another hundred thousand?"

"I'll quit right now."

He looked away. "I hope you've made the right choice, Hardman."

"You don't like it, you give me another one." I gave him time to answer but he didn't. "Tell me another way to go."

"I can't."

"Thanks for your confidence." I started for the door and turned back. "Hump and I are wondering why that guy on the phone is going to all that trouble to disguise his voice, if that's what he's doing."

"What does that mean?"

"That he knows you. That you might know him."

"The way he sounds, how the hell am I supposed to know?"

"Think about it." I nodded at Hump.

We went down the stairs past the shotgun soldier. I guess he was getting tired of spending time on the landing every time we dropped by. It was cold out there and I could see the condensation of his breath blowing at us as we passed.

CHAPTER FIVE

M arcy called a few minutes before eight the next morning. She did that now and then when she hadn't heard from me for a couple of days. She'd be ready for work, ready to leave her apartment and she'd get the impulse.

"Has the other girl left?"

"An hour ago. Couldn't stand the daylight."

"Was she pretty?"

"If you like the type," I said.

"What type is that?"

Like most of the conversations we had when I wasn't fully awake, I didn't know how serious she was. "A fat girl who smelled of feta cheese and olive oil."

"A Greek girl?"

"That's how she talked me into it. Came over and whispered in my ear. Asked me if I'd ever had a fat Greek girl who smelled of feta cheese and fresh pressed olive oil."

"What part of her smelled like feta cheese?"

"I don't remember."

"That answer is a lawyer's way around perjury."

Enough. "Marcy," I said, "the bed is empty."

"Whose fault is that?"

"Mine." There wasn't anything else I could say.

"I'll stop by at five. You be there."

I said I'd try.

"Do better than that, buster."

She slammed the receiver down. I got out of bed and made coffee and cooked up a couple of boiled eggs. I spent the rest of the morning bumping into myself all around the house. It was that kind of morning.

About noon, The Man called. "We had some luck."

"Not one minute too soon."

"Her name is Regina Clark. She goes back a ways with Ronny. Back before the picture was taken."

"How far back?"

"Five or six years. A lot of people remember Ronny out there. It's that way with the high rollers. Sometimes it's friendly watching and sometimes it isn't. One place my man showed the photo around, they remember Ronny and they remember the girl. You know how it is at the good hotels. Hookers hang around the bar until the dot of six. Then if they're not escorted they've got to get into their pumpkins and disappear. It's the rule."

I didn't know that but I said yeah like I did.

"One afternoon Ronny was in the bar. Got to talking with this young girl. Word is she looked old enough. The girl hustled him out of a few chips to play blackjack with. She was playing and it got past six P.M. and these two big security men come in, grab her hands and cuff them behind her. Ronny got pissed. Stormed over and said she was with him. He was raising all kinds of hell when they told him the girl was being hauled off for being underage. She was seventeen."

It sounded like Ronny. He could bellow and he was a sucker for lost people.

"Ronny got her released. He tried to help her."

"His kind of thing," I said.

"The girl was hard up and she didn't want to sell it and she didn't want to work at one of those pig ranches outside of town. Ronny staked her until she found a job. Used to see her when he was in town. Nobody cares about anybody's morals out there. Still, the word was that it was like a father and daughter thing."

"And she disappeared from Vegas a few months back."

"You know this already?"

"Guessed some of it."

"Girls float in and out of Vegas. Nobody keeps tabs. Close as my man could figure, it was anywhere from two to six months ago that she dropped out of sight. My man said he'd check closer if I thought it was worthwhile."

"Call him back. Find where she was staying. See if there's a forwarding address."

"I'm ahead of you. He's doing that now. He'll call me back in a couple of hours."

"It's opening up."

"How?" He didn't sound as sure as I did.

I wasn't sure and I didn't feel like bluffing. "After we find her I'll know."

Before I closed off the call, I said I'd be gone for an hour or so. If he didn't reach me, I'd call him.

At Cloudt's, the fancy food store on Peachtree, I had the butcher cut me a couple of sirloin steaks. Before I headed for the wine store next door, I wandered up and down the aisles looking at the exotic stuff on the shelves. In one section I found a jar with about four or five black ugly truffles in it. The price on it was $40. Since I'd never had a truffle before and didn't know what kind of taste it had, I passed it up, good bargain that it was.

I did buy a crusty wedge of Stilton and some ripe Anjou pears.

The Man called at three. No word from Vegas yet.

A few minutes before five, I unwrapped the meat and put the two steaks on a platter. I ground some fresh pepper on both sides of the meat and pressed the coarse pepper in.

Marcy charged in exactly at five. She gave the steaks only a glance in passing. "I want to talk to you, buster." She threw her purse on the sofa, kicked off her shoes and headed for the bedroom. I don't like pushy women, but I said, what the hell, and followed her.

It was short and violent, that lovemaking. Maybe it was what both of us needed. At the end of it she perched on an elbow and looked at me. "Feta cheese, huh?"

"Don't forget the olive oil."

By six-thirty, she'd made the salad and heated up the old black cast iron skillet. She dropped in half a stick of butter and one of the steaks. Just a minute or two on each side. I opened a bottle of Saint Julian and poured out two glasses. As soon as the first steak was done, I started on it while she seared hers.

We finished the last of the wine with the Stilton and the pears. When the call came, I took another pear with me and ate it while The Man talked.

"It was a lot of trouble. The Clark girl lived in three or four places those years in Vegas. When he reached the last one, he found she hadn't left a forwarding address with the super. There hadn't been any mail for her at the apartment. He took it to mean she'd filled out a forwarding address at the post office."

He was good, that man out in Vegas.

"He tried to work it with a clerk at the post office. No help there. The clubs might run Vegas but the clerk got scared and backed off."

Maybe he hadn't offered enough money.

"He had to start over. Back to the super. The super called the rental agency and got her bank reference. By the time he had that the banks had closed for the day. He knew I was pressing for the information so he went looking for someone with clout enough to call one of the bank vice-presidents. He hit it good this time. When Regina Clark closed out her checking account there were a couple of outstanding checks. She left enough in the account to cover the checks and she gave an address in Atlanta where the last statement could be mailed."

"Where?"

"An apartment on Briarcliff." He gave me the street number and the apartment number.

"I'll check it tonight."

"Call me."

I said I would. I dropped the pear stem in an ash tray and started getting dressed. Back in the kitchen I could hear the excessive, angry clatter of dishes in the sink. Marcy knew what the call meant. Damn. Before I left the bedroom, I called Hump.

"Busy?"

"This sweetmeat trim has been working on my bruises."

"I've got an address for the girl."

"Pick me up."

I leaned over the kitchen table and cut myself another crumbled wedge of Stilton. Marcy, her hands in the suds, looked over her shoulder at me. "That what I think it was?"

"Sorry."

"At least you won't be running around town all night, all horny."

I choked on the cheese. Marcy was learning how to talk bad.

I found the apartment without too much trouble. After we parked, we split up. A minute or so later Hump whistled. He'd found #23. There was light in the breezeway. No name tag in the metal frame on the door. I gave the doorbell a push or two and waited. No answer, so I walked down the stairs and looked at the windows to the apartment. The drapes were open and no light showed.

I was ready to head back to the car. At the top of the stairs, from the breezeway, Hump waved at me. I climbed the stairs. "Yeah?"

"Hear it?"

I could. The muffled beat of hard rock. I circled Hump and leaned against the door of apartment #24. It was coming from inside. I hit the doorbell a long burst.

As soon as the door opened, I got nostrils and a mouthful of the grass smoke. A tanned young man in a pair of tennis shorts, his chest bare, swayed in the doorway. "If you're fuzz, I give up."

"Don't surrender yet. We're not."

"Oh, shit." He twisted around and yelled over the music, "Betty, don't light the fucking incense. It's not the cops."

"The girl next door, do you know where she is?"

"Her?" His mouth drooped. "Way she acted you'd have thought it was gold and encrusted with jewels." He yelled into the apartment once more. "Betty, you remember me telling you about that stuck-up girl next door?"

"Fuck her," the girl inside said.

"You know where she is?"

"Gone. Moved out. Must have been scared I'd grab hold of that sweet little body of hers."

"When?"

"What's today?" He blinked at me.

"Thursday."

"Must have been Monday then."

"You here when she moved out? You see what moving company hauled her stuff?"

"Not me. It was during the day. I was off working. Have to keep Atlanta booming."

"Bob," the girl in the apartment shouted, "come back to bed."

He smiled. "Listen to my fans." He fumbled for the doorknob and pushed at the door. "Nice talking but I've got to go."

I wedged a shoe in the door opening. "You got a resident manager here?"

"Apartment 1."

I moved my shoe and he closed the door with a wham. I had another question. It floated up at me. I pushed the bell and braced myself.

The door opened only inches that time. "Look, it's been nice talking to you but I've got better—"

"One question and I'll leave you to it. The way you talk you tried to get close to the girl next door, right?"

"I tried to borrow a cup of gin from her." He laughed. "It's something I saw a guy do on TV one night."

"No luck, huh?"

"Frosty."

"But you didn't give up?" I could guess that. He was the type you'd have to use a bat on.

"I tried a time or two more."

"You find out what she did for a living?"

"Sure. I found out. Got to know enough to do the small talk."

"What?"

"She was a dance instructor. One of those places where people learn to dance. It wasn't Arthur Murray but it was one like that."

It meshed. It fitted. I backed away. "Have a good walk in the woods."

"What else." This time, after the slam died down, I heard the lock slip into place.

I dropped Hump off and drove home. I got the yellow pages and used the kitchen table as a desk. "Dance Instruction" covered a bit more than two pages. After a glancing down the listings, I used a felt-tipped pen to strike out the ones I thought we could bypass. Ballet and tap, belly dancing. From the look at Regina Clark, she didn't have the belly for the Mid-eastern.

Marcy mixed me a drink and watched while I assembled the list. All the downtown ones in the first group. The others according to the sections of town. When I'd written down the last one and pushed the pad aside, she came around the table and nibbled at my ear lobe. "Bedtime, Jim?"

"You staying?"

A whisper. "Yes."

"Bedtime."

We started with the downtown group. It might have been easier to split the list with Hump. Maybe, maybe not. I'd seen Regina Clark and he hadn't. And the trimmed-down photos didn't do the real, live woman justice. Not the way that brief look at her in the church entranceway had.

By noon, we'd run through the downtown group. Blanks all the way. We stopped for lunch and a couple of beers. Then grunting it up and starting over again.

It wasn't luck. It was footwork, touching the bases. Around three, at Broadview Plaza, we got the right one, The Buddy Parks Studio. It might have been in the second division, located as it was above an oriental supermarket, but they'd gone to a lot of expense and trouble to dress it up. Black wrought iron railing on the stairs that might have come from Charleston. A reception room that had about ten thousand dollars' worth of antiques. Just the desk, the sideboard and the love seat would have cost that much.

And a knockout of a receptionist. No way to price her. Five-two or so. A dark tan, light brown hair with a bit of frost in it and a body that made me think she'd robbed a couple of other girls and left them flat and fleshless to get what she had.

Must be businesslike. Mustn't look like I'm a bill collector. "I'd like to see Miss Regina Clark."

At the other places I'd gotten blank looks. Not here. The look read me, layer through layer down to my brand of underwear. "Do you have an appointment with Miss Clark?"

"Not exactly."

"I don't understand." But I think she did. I think she'd marked us down as trouble and drawn a line under us.

"We'd like to talk to Miss Clark about taking lessons."

"Both of you?" She tilted her head and looked at Hump.

"Just me," I said. "He can dance already."

"Miss Clark is busy right now. She is giving private instructions and the session won't be over for some time."

"We'll wait."

I backed away from the desk. The plaque on the front edge of the desk gave me her name. Miss Winters. Hump turned with me and we headed for the love seat. Just before we got there, I looked over my shoulder at Miss Winters. I could read the alarm on her face. Together we'd weigh almost five hundred pounds. Enough to shatter the fragile piece of furniture into stove wood.

I touched Hump on the arm and we walked over to a couple of molded plastic chairs. We smoked and waited. Ten minutes passed. Miss Winters stared at us. I met her eyes and blew smoke at her. Screw all that good-looking meat. Turn it over and it's all gray on the back.

Five minutes more. It got to her. She got up and rounded the desk. From the side, as she approached me, Hump looked over the merchandise.

"I'm sure Miss Clark won't be able to see you today. She's late now and she had another appointment in ten minutes."

"We'll wait."

"I can fill out a form with you and set up an appointment for the first of next week."

"I'd rather not."

"But I'm telling you—"

"We'll wait."

Hump stood up and stretched. "I'll fill out a form with you. Might be I could use some brush-up."

Miss Winters read that for what it really was and ignored Hump. "It won't do any good." She returned to the desk. When she was seated, to her left, there were a series of buttons. A call system. Eyes on us she pressed one down and said, "Miss Clark, there are two men out here to see you. I don't know who they are."

When she released the button and looked away, one eyelid twitched, like an involuntary wink. I stood up. I didn't like that last move.

"I'll walk back and meet her."

"You can't go back there."

"Watch me." I turned back to Hump. "Jolly this lady for me."

"Don't throw me in that briar patch," Hump said.

"And call Art at home. He won't be at the police department yet." I added that for Miss Winters. It would nail her to the floor for a few minutes.

Past the door with "STUDIOS" printed on it, I was in a wide hall. I could see four doorways, two to each side, and a doorway at the end with a red "EXIT" sign above it. The first door to the right was open. Empty. The door to the left was cracked slightly. A tall girl with platinum blonde hair was dancing groin to groin with a gray-haired business type. It was cool but he was sweating. What we used to call in the army a dry-hump.

One more bank of rooms to go. I was almost there when the door to the right opened and Regina Clark stepped out. "... want to see me later, I think ..." Then she saw me and broke off in mid-sentence. She turned to the side and a man passed her and faced me in the hall. He was in his late twenties. The boyish face that women seem to like, marred, I thought by a half-moon scar that almost formed a cleft in his chin.

"Miss Clark," I said, "I'm Jim Hardman."

"I don't have time. I have another—"

"I was a friend of Ronny's."

"I don't know … I don't know anybody named Ronny."

Pretty-boy wanted to score some points. "I don't think you ought to bother—"

"Butt out," I said.

He clenched his fists. Regina Clark touched his shoulder. "Jim, I don't think you ought to get involved."

His name was Jim too. For a second, I thought she was talking to me and it didn't make any sense.

He said, "I'll call the police."

"They're already on the way."

"Well …" It took some of the steam out of him.

"Go on." She gave him a gentle push. "I'll see you at the next lesson."

He brushed past me, still the outraged defender of young women. I watched him until he reached the door to the reception room, pushed the door open with a bang and stepped through. It closed behind him.

"So you don't know Ronny?"

"No."

"That's funny. I don't think Ronny ever would have said he didn't know you."

It broke her. Like I'd slammed a fist in her belly and knocked the breath out of her. She whirled, putting her back to me, and covered her face with her hands and began to cry.

Art hooked a foot on a chair and pulled it over until it faced the one where Regina Clark was seated. A cigarette in the corner of his mouth wagged at me. I passed behind him and closed the door to the studio. Art said, "You've been hard to find, Miss Clark. I hope there was a good reason."

"I was afraid."

"Of what?"

"I was afraid you'd think I had something to do with ... with what happened to Ronny."

"Running away didn't look good."

"I was leaving town tomorrow," she said.

I pushed away from the closed door. "Back to Vegas?"

A flick of her eyes, surprised that I knew. "Yes."

"It wouldn't have been far enough. You remember a picture you had taken at the Sands back in December of '72? Ronny kept a copy."

"It was my twenty-first birthday."

Art turned and hooked an elbow over the back of his chair. I could see he was in a bind. He wanted to know what I knew but he didn't want to admit in front of the person he was questioning that he didn't have all the facts.

"A security man I know in Vegas checked the picture back to you and it led us to the apartment on Briarcliff." I made a cut-hand gesture to Art. I'd explain it to him later, as much as I could without throwing The Man into the pot. "We know how you met Ronny and we know he helped you and we think he felt about you the way he might about real family."

I could see the tension falling away. "I thought the police might misunderstand."

"One thing was working for you. We didn't know you but we knew Ronny. It wasn't his style and he had style."

"He was the nicest man I ever knew. He wasn't like all those other men, the ..."

"Shakers and movers?"

She nodded. It was close enough. "If he wanted anything out of me, I never knew what it was."

"Friendship?" I said. It was a kind of love.

Art saw that she was about to break. He took time to offer her a smoke and light it for her. He waited until she had it under control before he went on. "When did you come to Atlanta?"

"Three months ago."

"Your idea or his?"

"Both, I guess. He knew I wasn't happy in Las Vegas. He kept telling me to come to Atlanta. And one day, when it was so bad I didn't think I could stand it any longer, I called him and he sent me a plane ticket."

"Anything special happen in Vegas?"

"No. It was the usual. A man I worked for started acting like working for him meant working under him."

"Tell us about Atlanta," I said.

She liked Atlanta. Ronny found her an apartment and he had a friend who had a friend and out of that had come the job at the dance studio. But she'd been surprised by a few things. Out in Vegas she'd thought Ronny was rich, the way he threw money around. As soon as she reached Atlanta, she realized that he was down on his luck. His apartment wasn't lavish and though he had money for most things, she knew it wasn't unlimited and she began to refuse the kind of financial help she'd been willing to take earlier.

"Last Friday night," I said.

Most weekends she spent at least one day with him. On Friday, she'd gone out to fix supper for him and she'd intended to stay all evening, watching TV or listening to music with him.

"The way you say it," Art said, "something was different this time."

"He said he had some work to do."

That would be the work on The Man's ledgers.

"Purvis, the resident manager, said he stopped by Ronny's apartment that night." Art turned to me. "What time did he say?"

"Seven o'clock. He was on the way to a bingo game."

"You were in the apartment then, Miss Clark?" Art said.

"I was in the kitchen making a salad."

I looked around for an ash tray. I couldn't find one, so I brought over the metal trash can. I placed it between Art and Regina Clark. I lit a smoke and backed away, circling until I was directly behind her. "What was supper?"

"Baked pork chops, asparagus and a tossed salad."

"You ate and then what?"

"I washed the dishes and cleaned up the kitchen. By then it must have been eight o'clock."

"You left then?"

She nodded and then she realized that, asking the question behind her, I couldn't see the nod. She said, "Yes."

Art said, "You left the Starlight Estates about eight. Where'd you go from there?"

"To my apartment on Briarcliff. I'd intended to spend the evening with Ronny, and I didn't have any other plans."

"Anyone see you there?" I leaned past her and dropped an ash in the trash can.

"I don't think so." She hesitated. "Yes, the man next door."

"Apartment 24?"

She looked over her shoulder at me. "I'd hardly taken my coat off when he knocked. He said he was stuck with some tickets to the Hawk game. If we hurried, we could get there for the second half."

"He high that night?"

"I don't know. Maybe he was."

Art reached out and took the short butt from Regina's fingers and mashed the coal out on the side of the trash can. "You know him, Jim?"

"Met him yesterday. He smokes like an old stove."

Art braced the pad on his knee. "His name?"

I shook my head.

"I think his name is Harris," Regina said.

"First name Bob," I added. I could still hear the strident voice of the girl yelling from the bedroom.

Art wrote it down. "I'll check this with him. He backs it up and you're clear."

"And you stayed home all evening?"

"Yes."

"Nobody called you, anything like that?"

"I don't have any friends in Atlanta."

"Stay around," I said. "You'll make a few."

I was watching Art's face. Puzzlement and dissatisfaction mixed on his face. Here he had his first good witness and the deadend signs were still up.

"There's one thing," Regina said. "I don't know if it matters."

"It might."

"I was thinking back over that last time with Ronny. Right before I left, he did something."

"Go on, Regina."

"It's probably not important."

"What happened?" Art sounded impatient.

"It was strange. I was standing in the kitchen doorway, putting on my coat, and I saw him move the sugar bowl and the salt and pepper shakers from the dining table and place them on the counter by the stove. Then he put the big ash tray from the living room in the center of the table."

She'd been right the first time. It wasn't important.

"And I think I saw a chip holder and a number of decks of cards on the kitchen counter."

"How many decks?"

"I just saw them out of the corner of my eye. But it might have been eight or ten decks."

"A poker game," I nodded at Art. "Ronny was having a play money party."

"But Wednesday was his poker night."

"Usually." I cut an eye toward Art. He knew it too. He'd heard it fall over. The deadend sign was down.

"Does that help?" She looked from me to Art. "I really want to help."

"I think it does." Art isn't one to bubble away. He gets a lot more distance out of understatement. Now it was wrap-up time for this interview. "Where are you staying now?"

"The Hotel Francis until tomorrow."

That was the low rent district. I couldn't see her fitting in there.

"You're going to have to stay a few more days," Art said.

I asked, "You short, Regina?"

The four or five beats of hesitation meant she didn't like answering me. "A little. I've got a plane ticket to Vegas and enough to keep me until I find a job."

"Marcy will put her up for a few days."

"I don't want to be any trouble..." she began.

"It's that," Art said to her, "or I'll have to find some reason to hold you."

"Marcy's my woman. She's not a jailer."

"And too good a woman for the fat man here."

"All right," she said, "if she doesn't mind."

"She won't."

Art stood up. "I'll need a full statement tomorrow. I'll call you here."

"I've given my notice. Today's the last day."

"Marcy's place then."

Out in the reception room, Hump had done a bit more than jolly Miss Winters. They were head to head and he was feeding her some candy nonsense. She was buying about half of it. Regina left us and went into the ladies rest room. I walked Art down the flight of stairs to the street level.

"I could be wrong but the girl seems straight."

He buttoned his topcoat and turned up the collar. "My feeling too." He opened the door and the cold wind sliced in. "What if Marcy won't put her up?"

"She will." I grinned at him. "I'll give her a choice. Either she puts Regina up or I will."

I used the desk phone to call Marcy's office. I didn't have to use the either/or thing with her. She said she'd come by my place after work. I replaced the receiver and stood back and listened to some of Hump's con and candy. It was some of his best.

"How's the briar patch?"

"Makes me itch."

"Scratch it," I said.

An eyelid drooped at me. "This girl's going to have a drink with me."

I heard the question in that. I got out my key ring and unclipped my car key. "Keep in touch."

We drove to my place in Regina's Pinto. On the way I offered to stop by the Hotel Francis and pick up her things. She said she'd rather wait until the next day. She could pick them up on her way to or from the police department.

That out of the way, she said very little. I gave her directions to my place. Left turn here, right turn there, and I guess I got so relaxed that I didn't notice she'd been studying me.

"You knew Ronny for a long time?"

"Almost twenty years."

"That's odd. He never mentioned you."

"Not really. He was a gambler. I wasn't. The worlds don't touch much." I knew where she was heading. I decided to spread it out for her. "I didn't know about his hard luck. Not until after he was dead. If I'd known, I'd have tried to help him. Maybe you know. He was a close man. The few times I saw him in the last few years he looked like big money. I didn't feel like I belonged."

"And yet you're trying to find out what happened to him."

"It's simple enough. To him, maybe I never got past being the kid he'd helped out in a game once. Maybe. But how you feel about other people isn't dependent on how you think they feel about you."

For some reason I didn't understand, what I'd said closed her up again. She fell into *yes* and *no* and it was a deep pit and finally I gave up and left her there.

By six, Marcy and Regina were on a first-name basis. We had a couple of drinks and a little later they left, Regina following her in the Pinto. I washed the glasses and refilled the ice trays and I wandered around the house, running into small pockets of their perfume. Hers here and Marcy's there. After a time I couldn't tell which was which.

CHAPTER SIX

The agony wasn't long. After an hour or so, the perfumes blended in with the other closed-in winter smells. I brewed up a cup of instant coffee and carried it into the bedroom. I dialed the department and got Art on the line.

"You got the photos taken at Ronny's apartment?"

"Wait a minute."

While he was gone, I could hear a hunt-and-peck typist doing his two words a minute off in the background.

"Got them," he said.

"Any of the kitchen?"

"One."

"The table in the kitchen set for a poker game?"

"No. No cards. No chip holder. Looks like a sugar dish, salt and pepper shakers, and a napkin holder."

"That doesn't bother you, Art?"

"Because of the girl's story? Sure it does."

"Look in the inventory of the apartment's—"

"I'm ahead of you," Art said. "I've checked the list. No chip holder on it and only two decks of cards. One used, the other with the seal intact. But they weren't in the kitchen. They were in a bureau drawer in the bedroom."

"Not enough cards for a game."

"So how do you see it, Jim?"

"Say they play a few hands. When they start cleaning up the mess, after Ronny's dead, they have to worry about the cards. Could have left the chip holder except for the fact it'd point to a game. Too many prints on the cards so they'd have to be taken away. So they just dump the whole mess in a sack and cart it away."

"Or," Art said, "they didn't play at all."

"Huh?"

"The poker game's just an excuse. Maybe they just walk in and get down to the other business. When that's done, they've got a dead man on their hands. They're combing through the apartment and they get to the kitchen. They see the chip holder and the unbroken decks of cards. They know if the police see those it'll read poker game. Have to haul those off."

"Or there was never a poker party planned in the first place. It was a cocktail party and they were going to show the Candy Barr blue movie."

"Screw you."

I told him I'd get back to him in a day or two.

I had a sip of coffee and tried Hump's number. No answer. I watched TV for a time and then dialed the number again. Still no answer. Hump and that fox, Miss Winters. All that body. He'd run her to ground in some hole other than his own bed.

"Jim?"

I got up on an elbow and looked at the dial of the clock on the night table. It was two-ten A.M.

"Yes, Hump?"

"It's messy over here."

"What? Where are you?" My head wasn't working. I could blame that on about three shots of J&B.

"It's Betty Winters."

"What about her?"

"She's dead in the doorway. I just called Art over at the police."

"How'd it happen?"

"I was on the crapper. She was making drinks. Guess the doorbell rang. Soon as she opened the door somebody shot her a few times."

"How many times?"

"It sounded like three but I can't be sure. The one time in the face was enough."

"Dead?"

"Dead, Jim? She's blood pudding."

He gave me the address. It was one of the old apartment houses out Peachtree N.E., around 17th Street, a few blocks before the two parts of Peachtree merge and become Peachtree Road.

I got dressed and I was at the front door before I realized I didn't have a car. Hump had it. I had to wait twenty-five minutes for a cab. It gave me time to have a weak cup of coffee.

"Door was on the chain," Art said. He nodded his head at Hump who was seated in a rope-bottomed chair. "According to Hump the light was on in the bedroom, out here in the living room, and on in the kitchen where she was mixing drinks."

"She was back and side lighted," I said.

"And maybe front lighted from the hall," Art said.

I leaned over Hump and shook out a cigarette and lit it for him. "Who the hell would want—?" I didn't finish it. I let it trail off and die.

A plainclothes cop with Art, an older man with a twitchy rat's face, leaned in. He'd been listening. "A jealous boyfriend. He's waiting outside. Sees his girl come in with company. Gets mad and kills her."

Some people piss me. All the first level, slow-headed shit. "You got the name of this boyfriend?"

He shrugged. "We can ask around. It'll be the way I said."

"Do that, Bert," Art said. "Do it door-to-door. See who heard the shots. See if anybody saw anybody leaving right after the shots."

"Sure, Art."

He swaggered out of the apartment. Art watched him go. "I think Bert ass-kissed his way out of uniform."

Hump lifted his head. The smoke from the cigarette in the corner of his mouth drifted up into one eye. He squinted. "It wasn't her they wanted dead. It was me."

"Why?"

Art waited for Hump to answer. He didn't and after the silence lasted for a minute or so I knew that he wasn't going to. I said, "A couple of nights ago Hump and I dropped in to see Mort Heppler."

"Heppler? That's high class. Why?"

"He and Ronny were pals. Word was Mort and Ronny still saw each other. Nothing came of the talk but Hump and a curly-haired dude named Tony Mitchell got their fur up. Ended up in a boxing and butting contest in the parking lot outside the Dogwood Lounge."

Art looked at Hump. "Still puffy, huh?"

"A bit."

"How'd the fight come out?"

"Hump scraped his plow."

"What does Mitchell do for Heppler?" Art asked.

"I think he carries a piece for Heppler."

"You see him carrying?"

I shook my head. I was thinking along with Art. First step was to find out if Mitchell had a permit. If so, for what kind of iron. If not, he could make trouble for Mitchell if he found him carrying without a permit. "He looks the type."

Art grunted. "I'd like for you to put that silly statement down in writing."

While Hump got his coat, I walked over to the bedroom and looked in. A frilly blue place, pillows on the floor and the sheets looked like a dozen or so wildcats had fought a war in the center of the bed.

"Thanks for not asking how it was."

I tossed a pillow past him. It landed on the sofa next to him. On the way back from the girl's apartment, I'd said he might as well spend the night at my place and he hadn't argued.

"I don't remember ever asking," I said. "Not even about the live ones."

"That's right. Sorry."

"But somebody else did?"

"Not in so many words," he said.

"Who?"

"A redneck cop. First one to arrive. Took one look at her and one look at me. He wrote her off as a pig who sold it for a living."

"Liked her, huh?"

"Seemed a nice girl after you got past a lot of that woman crap. After you got past the fact that everybody wanted her ass and what that did to her."

I stretched and yawned. "See you in the morning. You know where the booze is."

"You're thinking Mitchell?"

"If the shots were meant for you, he's the obvious one."

"Like they used to say..."

I waited.

"If it was Mitchell he'd better give his soul to God—"

I finished it for him. "... because his ass belongs to you."

I didn't fall asleep right away. I could hear him prowling around the living room and the kitchen. I heard bottle and glass noise and the old springs in the sofa creaking.

It was ten when I woke up. Hump was already gone. My car was still in the driveway. It meant, I guess, that he'd called a cab from right next to my bed and I'd been so far under that I hadn't heard him.

I dressed and called The Man while the water heated for the instant coffee.

"I don't expect the call until later this afternoon," he said as he came on the line.

"It's not that." I lit a smoke and coughed on the first drag from it. "I need to see Mort Heppler again."

"This time of day?"

"The sooner the better. The pot's boiling."

He called back in ten minutes. Under some protest, Mort Heppler would see me at noon at the Bayside Club. "And wear a coat and tie so you don't make him look bad."

I stubbed out the smoke and made a cup of coffee. I waited a few minutes and called Marcy.

"Everything all right over there?"

"Fine. She's a nice girl."

"Let me talk to her."

"She's not here. She's gone to check out of the hotel and pick up her things."

"Art call her?"

"No."

Nothing strange about that. I guess she needed a change of clothes.

"When am I going to see you, buster?"

"Soon. Maybe tonight."

"Promise?"

I said I crossed my heart and hoped to die. As soon as I put the receiver down, I decided that considering what had happened the night before, it wasn't the best kind of promise I could have made.

The Bayside Club isn't one of the top five in Atlanta. It looks good enough from the outside. Something like Mount Vernon would look if it had been built by a troop of hippie carpenters. The lawn in the spring and summer is as large and as well-kept as any nine-hole golf course in the city.

It's as exclusive as any other Atlanta social club. Membership is held down to a hundred families. For the favored there is hand-ball and tennis and swimming. Bars and dining rooms and game rooms where the gentlemen can play a few hands of cards with-out fear that police will interrupt the game.

But it is second rate. It doesn't carry the prestige of a club like the Piedmont Driving Club. In a newspaper write-up Bayside Club means new money, money acquired in the last fifty years. The Piedmont Driving Club means old money, dollar bills that have been turning over and over since before Sherman marched through and held the first citywide barbecue.

I had to wait at the desk while the steward sent one of his flunkies into the plush bowels of the club. It appeared that Mort Heppler had forgotten to leave my name on the day's guest book. Like hell, he'd forgotten.

"This way." The flunky returned and led me through the huge, high-ceilinged reading room, over thick carpets and past old wooden panels they must have bought right off the wall of some mansion in Europe.

He stopped in the doorway that separated the reading room and a small bar. Mort Heppler and another younger man sat across from each other at a table some distance from the bar, away from any ears that might have a backward turn to them.

As I approached Heppler's table, the man seated across from him saw me first. He got to his feet and gave me a slow look before he backed his way to a bar stool. I tagged him as paid help. I don't know how he tagged me.

I stood behind a chair and waited for Heppler to invite me to sit down. He took his time. "Have a seat, Hardman."

As soon as my butt hit the chair bottom, a waiter trotted over.

"I'm having sherry," Heppler said.

"A beer," I said and, because it looked fancy enough, added, "A Beck's if you have it."

The waiter trotted back a few seconds later with a bottle of Beck's and a pilsner glass. Unchilled.

I poured half a glass and sipped it. Mort Heppler, looking as frail and near death as the last time I saw him, toyed with his sherry glass.

"You don't seem too pleased to see me today." I said.

"I like to keep my business and my social life apart."

"I couldn't wait until your business hours."

Heppler said, "Perhaps you'll tell me what's so pressing."

I eased around in my chair and looked at the bodyguard at the bar. He was drinking straight Coke and watching me, every move I made. "What happened to your other boy?"

"Who was that?" He wasn't going to volunteer anything.

"Mitchell."

"Tony? He quit."

"Quit or was fired?"

He spread his hands. "It was a bit of both. After the incident in the parking lot, I thought he might not be suited to the profession he'd chosen and he decided he needed a vacation."

"You know where he is now?"

"No."

"Where did he live when he worked for you?"

"In the guest house," Heppler said. "What had been a gardener's cottage at one time."

"He move out?"

He nodded. "The day he quit."

"Leave a forwarding address?"

"Are you sure this is important? I'm not sure Tony would want to see you after the other night."

I leaned forward, perhaps a bit abruptly. Behind me I could hear the heels hit the floor. "Last night somebody tried a hit on Hump. They killed a girl instead. Hump's out looking for Mitchell now."

"And you're worried about Tony?"

"Not at all." I looked over my shoulder at the bodyguard. He'd edged close to me. "Call him off."

"It's all right, Bob."

I kept my eyes on him until he was seated at the bar again. "I'm not worried about Mitchell at all. Screw him in the nose. Fuck him in the ear."

"Then it's your partner you're worried about?"

"It comes to killing you can do time for offing low life, just like you'd do for a preacher."

"Evans is no concern of mine."

"A beating in a parking lot. Is that worth a killing?"

"People kill for a lot of things. They kill for less than a bad beating."

I decided to drop the handkerchief and see if anybody'd pick it up. "The Wednesday poker games, was Mitchell there?"

"Of course."

"Watching you or playing?"

"He sat in a few times," Heppler said, "when we were a chair short."

"New news for you," I said. "The night Ronny was butchered he was set up for a game. Chips and cards."

"That's the Grand Canyon you're trying to jump now."

"Where was Mitchell that Friday night?"

"I don't know. In the guest house, I suppose."

"You don't know?"

"Tony took a night off now and then."

"And that Friday was a day off."

"I'll have to check my records."

"Bull."

"All right, he was off that night," Heppler said. "There was a girl he'd met at the Lounge. A divorcee, I think."

"Her name?"

He shook his head. "The night bartender might know."

I made the circle. I reached back in the jumble that was the beginning of the conversation. "I need Mitchell's address."

"He didn't give it to me." He sighed, a long rattling flutter that sounded like one lung might go. "Okay. He asked if my driver could drop some of his things off for him. The driver said he took them to the Executive Motel downtown."

"Thanks." I poured down some of the Beck's.

"You really think he had something to do with what happened?"

"To Ronny? I don't know."

"You're raking a lot of hay for somebody who isn't sure of much."

I shrugged that off. "I need one more favor from you."

"You can ask it. I think the favor box is empty."

"I need a list of everybody who played in the Wednesday games."

"I'm not sure I can make such a list," Heppler said.

"Can't or won't?"

"I'll have to think about it."

"Look at it this way, Mr. Heppler. Everything I heard said, Ronny lost his poker nerve a couple of years back. The only game he took cards in was the Wednesday one. Now, suddenly, he's having a Friday game at his place. Tell me, where'd he find the players?"

"You think he found them at my table."

"Tell me somewhere else."

"Old poker friends, people he hadn't played with for years."

"Those ghosts," I said. "I'll check the real ones first."

Heppler drained the last of his sherry. "I'll think about it."

"I'll drop by the Dogwood tonight."

"That might be too early."

"Don't take this as a threat. Think of it as a possibility. You know Art Maloney?"

"By reputation," Heppler said.

"He's working on the killings. He could ask you for the names."

"Bob." Heppler tilted his head toward me.

Leather heels struck the floor. A quick step toward me. I looked over my shoulder at him. He was close, one hand out, cupped to clamp on my shoulder.

"No hands," I said to him.

The hand straightened. He flexed it.

"Bob, show Mr. Hardman out. I wouldn't want him to lose his way."

I stood up. "What's a good time tonight? Nine o'clock?"

Heppler didn't answer.

"Nine o'clock then."

I left the bar. The hired help dogged my steps through the reading room, past the steward's desk and out the front door into the cold early afternoon. He stopped on the steps, blowing his frosty breath at me.

On the drive into town, I wondered if Hump was one step ahead of me or one step behind.

I parked in the motel lot. The motel was built on a narrow strip of land, in the shape of a clothespin. Three floors high. There was space for about fifty cars in the narrow courtyard. Getting out of the car I could see the maid's laundry cart on the second level.

I was on the way to the motel office when I heard a car door slam behind me.

"Jim." I looked around and saw Hump walking toward me. "He's not in."

"You sure?"

"I tried the door a few times."

"Which room?"

"34."

"Where is it?"

Hump turned and pointed up to the second level. I followed the angle and settled on a room a few doors down from where the laundry cart was.

"The maid clean it yet?"

Hump shook his head. "Heading that way now."

"The maid black?"

"Yeah."

"You jolly her then. See if we can buy five minutes in there."

I waited in front of room 34 while he eased his way down the breezeway and ducked into the room where the maid was working. He was in there about five minutes. When he came out, he was followed by a tiny little black woman who must have been about sixty.

"You wouldn't lie to me, would you, son?"

"Of course not, Reba."

She dug out a master key. She nodded at me as I stepped away from the doorway. After fitting the key into the lock she gave the empty courtyard another look. "You could get me fired."

"From this job?" Hump shrugged.

Reba laughed and unlocked the door. She stepped away. "I ain't got time to stay here with you."

"Five minutes," Hump said.

"I'll be back in ten."

It was 20th century motel plastic inside, so standard that a room in Georgia was exactly like one in California. The bed hadn't been slept in, the sheets and blanket in place and the pillows fluffed up. On the dresser a pad on which there was a plastic ice bucket and about a half bottle of a bar scotch. Hump stopped at the closet while I walked back to the bathroom. There was an electric razor on the shelf above the sink, a bottle of sandalwood cologne, a tube of paste and a toothbrush. The shower stall was empty.

I backed out of the bathroom. "Find anything?"

"The closet's full. Mitchell spends a lot on threads."

"Suitcases?"

"Five or six."

"Check them." I stood behind him and he pulled the cases out and passed them back to me. The first three were empty, I could tell that from the weight. The fourth felt empty too but when I shook it I could hear something slide around in it. I carried it to the bed and tried the locks. Locked. It would make for a messy look-around but I didn't know any other way. I got out my key ring and fingered through them until I found a sturdy one that didn't fit anything that I could remember, I used the edge of the key to pry around the locks until I sprung them. It was an inexpensive suitcase or it might not have worked.

Behind me, Hump checked the last suitcase. "Empty."

He reached the bed about the time I broke the second lock. I lifted the top of the suitcase and reached in. There it was. It was a stack of xerox copies about an inch and a half thick. The first page told me all I needed to know. It was a copy of The Man's ledger. Only one copy; I made sure of that before I closed the suitcase. "Stack them back the way they were."

I unbuttoned my coat and let my belt out a notch. I stuffed the xerox pages down the front of my pants until it was a kind of breast plate. I drew my coat over it and fastened it. Now, if I didn't have to bend over, I might make it.

We were out on the breezeway when Reba returned.

❧ ❧ ❧

Hump was parked in my driveway when I got there. I parked out on the street so I wouldn't block him. Once inside the house, I handed him the copy of the ledger and went into the bedroom. When I got through to The Man I said, "Any call yet?"

"No."

"When you get it play it close." I told him about the copy we found at Mitchell's motel room. "Make sure they've really got a copy of the ledger."

"How?"

Hump brought me a beer. I sipped at it. "Pick some page at random and have them read the figures off to you."

"And if they can't?"

"Then I've found the only copy there is."

"And if they can?"

"You'd better get the money together."

"It's ready now."

I told him I'd drop the copy by later in the day.

"Don't lose it, Hardman."

"Not a chance."

Hump was watching Roller Derby on the TV I sat down and drank my beer. "This question came to me, Hump."

"Ask it."

"How'd you find Mitchell's motel before I did?"

"I bought myself this Arco book on how to be a private detective."

"It help much?"

He shook his head. "And then I found the doorman at the Dogwood Lounge and scared the shit out of him."

"He remember you?"

"Like a nightmare," Hump said.

I left Hump to his TV. I undressed and slept for a couple of hours.

❧   ❧   ❧

It was seven-thirty when we got to The Man's apartment. The Man was seated at the table in the kitchen. Spread out around him were ten or twelve cartons of take-out food from one of the Chinese restaurants. One of The Man's soldiers was playing waiter for him.

"Like Chinese? Have some."

I showed him the xerox copy of the ledger and placed it on the kitchen counter behind him. Hump lifted one of the cartons with spareribs and passed it to me. I took one and he took one.

"No call yet."

"Might not be one." I peeled the meat from the bone and dropped the bone in the trash can. When I turned back, Hump offered me an egg roll. "If our luck holds that might be the only copy."

"You think Mitchell is our man?"

"I doubt it. His head doesn't carry the right kind of weight. The fight with Hump wasn't smart. It drew attention to him."

"Then he was a spear carrier." The Man waved a greasy hand at the soldier who was playing waiter. "Get two plates."

"Not for us. We'll nibble." I found the roast pork and forked out a thick slice. "We'll try to find Mitchell. I want to know where he got the copy of the ledger."

"Only one way he could have got it. He's in it up to his ears."

"Likely," I said.

"Sit down and eat. There's plenty."

I'd been watching the black as he moved around the table, pouring The Man's hot tea or changing plates for him. I realized that he planned to make his meal from the leftovers. It was in the blank stare he gave us while we nibbled. It soured it for me and I found a paper napkin and wiped my fingers.

"We've got to head out."

"You'll call later?"

"When we get the chance. Maybe around ten."

We ate at Eng's, the Chinese restaurant on the Strip. We passed up the ribs and the egg rolls and ordered the main courses.

Exactly at nine, I parked in the lot next to the Dogwood Lounge. The doorman saw us and backed away from the entrance. He moved so far back that he had one foot in the gutter.

"Heppler expecting us?"

"He didn't say."

Hump reached the door first and swung it open. I turned and went back to the doorman. "You see Mitchell today?"

"Not a sign of him."

"But you'd tell me if you had?"

He didn't answer. He wasn't afraid of me. It was Hump who gave him nightmares.

It was a larger crowd. It was the Saturday, let's screw our way into Sunday, bunch. Opposite the bar I stopped and leaned toward Hump so I'd be heard over the noise. "Try the bartender. See if you can find out a name and an address for the divorcee Mitchell spends time with."

Hump wasn't sure of me. "You handle it back there?"

"Give me ten minutes. If I'm not back come looking for me."

Heppler's new man, the one he called Bob, stood with his back to the office door. Either he spent a lot of time that way or he'd been expecting me. A few feet away from him I opened my coat and showed him my waistband was empty.

"I'm supposed to talk to you," he said.

"Talk away."

"He doesn't want to see you."

"After I came all this way?" I gave him my best hurt look. "All I want is the list I came for."

He opened his coat. He wore a dark green vest under the jacket. While he tried to stare me down, he dug a couple of fingers into the vest pocket and hooked a piece of paper. He passed it to me. I opened it and found five names and addresses typed on it. I didn't know any of the five.

"Thank him for me." I refolded the paper and put it in my topcoat pocket.

"I haven't finished talking."

"Spit it out."

"Mr. Heppler said to tell you he saw you those times as a favor for a friend. But he doesn't find you amusing any more. And the cop smell is still on you."

"It must be hard to wash off."

"It never washes off."

"He tell you to say that?"

"I threw it in myself...free."

"If it's free, you can shove it."

He didn't blink. "He said you've run the welcome into the ground. You're not to come back here."

"What does that mean?"

"It means," he said, "you come back and I'll have to be rough."

I grinned at him. I gave him a two-fingered salute that probably confused him. I went into the bar and found Hump.

"Do any good?"

I patted my topcoat pocket. "Yeah. And you?"

He nodded. "It cost a five."

Hump was driving. "It's still early. Where first?"

"I think we need the low comedy."

"Huh?"

"Mitchell's girlfriend."

"The bartender said she hasn't been in for a couple of nights."

"Name?"

"May Foster."

"Address?"

"Virginia Avenue. The better part of it." He caught a red light. He grinned. "The exact instructions he gave me..."

"Yeah?"

"...give me the idea he's made the trip a time or two."

Off Monroe and up Virginia until we passed Highland. Hump slowed then. He seemed to be looking for a certain house rather than a street number. "There." He parked across the street and we got out.

It was a narrow brick house, two floors with the brown trim that could be called gingerbread or phony Tudor or whatever. The yard was lit by a street lamp. It was a neat yard with the plants and shrubs protected by plastic against this hard part of the winter.

On the walk Hump said, "Selling insurance this time of night?"

"Not today. And you'd better stay back here. And don't do any evil grinning. These southern girls have a black nightmare. One look at you and she'll yell rape."

"Up you, white man."

But he stopped halfway up the walk. I went up the steps to the porch and rang the doorbell. After a minute or so, the porch light went on and I could see a pale thin face staring out at me.

"What do you want?"

"Mr. Heppler sent me."

"Who?"

"Mort Heppler. I've got a message for Tony."

"For Tony?" I heard a lock snap. "He didn't say—"

"Lady," I said, "when Mort Heppler wants a message delivered I've got to deliver it."

"He's not here."

"Where can I find him?"

"You can leave the message with me and I'll see that he gets it."

"It's not that kind of message. It's for Tony, nobody else."

"Are you alone?"

I looked over my shoulder at Hump. "Got a driver with me."

"He can't come in."

"I don't think he wants to."

She opened the door just enough for me to slide through sideways. She slammed it shut and flipped a lock. In the dim light of the hallway I got my impression of her. About mid-thirties, wispy thin blonde hair, a slim body but with a high rump showing under the robe and larger breasts than her narrow shoulders ought to have to carry around.

At the end of the narrow hallway it flared out into a living room. The sofa needed recovering and the matching easy chair had the shine of use on the arms. I made my guess that this was the furniture left from the marriage.

"You didn't tell me your name." She turned and the light caught the shine in the luminous eyes. The way she wouldn't hold my stare told me something else. How vulnerable she was. Like she was saying to me or to every man she met: tell me you love me or admire my mind and anything is possible.

"Bob," I said.

"Bob what?"

"It doesn't matter."

"Well, Bob, I know where Tony is but I'm not supposed to tell anyone."

"We tried the motel," I said.

"He's not there, not since yesterday."

"Tell me where I can reach him."

"I can't."

"I'm from Heppler."

"It doesn't matter."

I faced her squarely, some hardness in my voice. "I don't have time to argue with you."

Either she was stronger than I thought or she knew how to bluff. "I don't have much time. I'm going out."

"You got paper and an envelope?"

"Yes."

I watched the high rump bounce under the robe as she walked into a room off to the left. I could see enough of it to know it was a dining room. She returned a few seconds later with a sheet of paper and an envelope.

I sat down on the sofa and placed the paper on the coffee table. I wrote: "Mort wants to know what you did with the key to the washroom. He is getting tired of going to the service station down the street." Then, in case she opened the letter, I added: "Use code 3." I didn't sign it. I folded the sheet and stuffed the envelope and sealed it. I carried it over to her. "He ought to get this right away."

Her nod didn't mean much. Not yes or no or maybe.

At the door I said, "Sorry to butt in on you this way."

"It's all right."

She closed the door behind me and locked it. Hump wasn't on the walk. I crossed the street and found him in the car, the engine running and the radio tuned to WPLO, the country-western station. As Hump pulled away from the curb, I looked back. The porch light was still on.

"Turn around and come back. We'll wait her out."

Down the street until we found a driveway. Then back, cutting his lights as we coasted to a stop on the same side of the street as May Foster's house, about half a block away. Hump tapped the car radio. "You been listening to this? Country-western's gone crazy. Now they're admitting redneck girls screw."

Thirty minutes. I thought I'd missed it and read her wrong. Forty minutes. I considered giving it up. May Foster, at the forty-five minute mark, came out of the house and walked quickly to the tan Ford station-wagon in the driveway. After a couple of minutes of warm-up, with exhaust pluming behind the Ford, she headed away from us, toward the intersection of Virginia and Highland.

Hump gave her half a block and followed. Until Monroe the traffic was thin. After that Hump worked his way up, letting a couple of cars play sandwich meat. At Monroe and Ponce de Leon she stayed in the center lane and caught the red light.

On the other side of Ponce de Leon what had been Monroe would become Boundary. "Guess," I said to Hump.

"Downtown. Maybe a hotel."

"Wrong guess."

At Georgia Baptist Hospital, May Foster did a tight left into a parking lot. I ducked down and Hump went past. By the time Hump found a place to turn around and we approached the parking lot, she had crossed the street and was heading up the walk to the entrance.

"You," I said. Hump stopped and got out. He crossed the street at a trot. I got behind the wheel and pulled into the same lot where May Foster had parked.

After a time it got cold in the car. I kicked over the engine. The radio was still on WPLO and I let it stay there. I heard about eight or ten songs. All those country studs wasting away for love. All those nasal women hurting. In some ways they still didn't have the sex thing down straight yet.

Hump came out first. He stood at the curb and looked in both directions. I got out and walked to the street and got his attention. He huffed his way across to me and we walked to the car and got in.

"Funny thing," Hump said.

"Yeah?"

"Mitchell's been in the hospital since about midnight last night."

"She bite him?"

"Nothing like that. Talked to this black nurse. Seems he says he fell down in his shower and broke both his thumbs. Said he'd been drinking some."

"That wide receiver for Cincinnati, what was his name?"

"That was on artificial turf," Hump said.

"So he's not our man for the killing last night?"

"Not unless he's learned to fire a piece with his big toe."

"He doesn't have that much talent." I looked back across the street at the hospital. "He tucked away for the night?"

Hump shook his head. "Checking out now."

CHAPTER SEVEN

About an hour passed before May Foster stepped out and held the door while Tony Mitchell turned sideways to step through the entranceway. I watched their awkward progress. A topcoat, unbuttoned, rested on his shoulders. His hands, with casts that seemed to reach from his wrists down past the knuckles, were held away from his body, like any touch would set off some kind of pain.

The wind was strong out on the street. Before they stepped off the curb, a gust blew the topcoat from one shoulder. Without thinking he reached up for it. Then his hands dropped and May Foster leaned across him and pulled the topcoat back into place.

I stayed back and let them signal their moves to us. Obvious that they weren't heading back toward her apartment on Virginia. Going toward downtown Atlanta, hitting Peachtree and heading north.

"The motel," I said. It was my guess for the night.

"You want to put a nickel on that?"

"But he's not going to stay there. He probably can't pee by himself."

Near Peachtree and Baker. In the lane that would take her out the northwest branch of Peachtree. "Gone after the copy of the ledger," Hump said.

"A dime on that?"

Hump grunted. Sometimes making a bet with him you weren't sure you had booked the bet until he paid off or he held out a hand for payment.

The stationwagon turned in at the Executive Motel. Hump slowed, giving them a minute, and then he pulled in after them. Dim and dark in the narrow parking area, the only light from the low wattage bulbs on the walkways. There was a space about six cars in on the left. I pointed at it and Hump swung the wheel and eased in, about a skin thickness from taking paint off a VW van.

I looked at my watch. Ten after eleven. A Saturday night gone to hell.

Mitchell stood under a light on the ground level walkway in front of the space where the stationwagon was parked. May had gone back to the car for her purse. Heads almost together she opened the purse and took out a wad of bills. He held up his right hand, palm out, and she placed the wad of money against the cast part and watched until she was sure that the fingers closed over it. She said something and after he answered she dug down into the right hand topcoat pocket and brought out the key to the motel room.

She went toward the stairs that would take her up to the second level. He called after her. She leaned over the stair railing to answer him. He shook his head and whirled away. He passed between the Ford stationwagon and a Toyota, doing a sideways crab, and walked down the driveway toward where we were parked. Headed, I thought, for the motel office.

"Checking out," I said to Hump.

Hump nodded before he ducked his head and placed it against the wheel. Taking that as a signal I leaned my head against the dashboard. It was quiet enough to hear his leather heels on the drive, approaching and opposite us and then going away.

I pushed away from the dash and watched Mitchell. The stiff, almost uncoordinated walk. Not like that night in the parking lot beside the Dogwood Lounge. More like the pain from his hands threw his whole body out of sync.

A ripple of headlights on low beam brushed the back of my car. It was past before I knew it was there. Hardly any sound from the engine, like it might be coasting. A blue 1973 Nova.

Mitchell felt the lights and moved out of the drive off to the right, his head still straight ahead. The Nova was abreast of Mitchell when it stopped. Mitchell turned in the direction of the car. He approached the Nova and when he was about a step away, he ducked his head, about to lean in at window level. He didn't get that far.

The first shot hit him in the mouth. The second shot under the chin as he fell away.

No iron on me. I hit the door handle a slam and pushed it open. I yelled at Hump, "Follow him."

Out in the cold wind, I slammed the car door and jumped away. Hump backed out. By the time he got it turned, the Nova had reached the street and peeled to the right. Hump burned rubber.

I could still smell the mixture of powder and rubber when I squatted over Mitchell. There wasn't much left of his face except for bone and blood mush. Probably he was dead by the time he hit the asphalt.

Behind me, leaning against the second floor railing, May Foster screamed and screamed. It had the piercing quality of a World War II air raid siren. It lasted until she ran out of breath.

"And you two were doing what?"

I was out of the wind now. In the motel room. Mitchell's clothing was thrown in all directions. The suitcases were open and spread about the room, the sheets ripped from the bed and the mattress half off the bed. Somebody had done an angry look-around since we were there earlier in the day.

"I told you once," I said.

Art said, "Tell me another time. I'm slow."

Saved by the uniformed cop who opened the motel door. "Another guy who said he saw the shooting."

Hump walked in. One look at me and he spread his hands and shook his head. "Lost him."

I caught my breath while Hump told Art about the chase down Peachtree and out Whitehall. He caught a red light and couldn't run it because there was traffic coming off Alabama. Ran it as soon as he could but by then the Nova had buried itself on one of the side streets.

"License?"

Hump shook his head. "I didn't even get close enough to see how many were in the car."

"One," I said.

Art lifted his eyebrows at me.

I explained. "Had to be. It was the way it was handled. The Nova stopped. The driver edged over, rolled down the window on the passenger side, tolled Mitchell over. Wouldn't have had to do that if there'd been a shooter in the passenger seat."

"Sure kill?" Art said.

"It was anyway," I said.

It was almost one o'clock before we got away from the Executive Motel. May Foster was at Grady, sedated so that Art couldn't talk to her until the next day. Not that I figured she could tell him much. Art had a wild hair with barbs on it as far as I was concerned. He knew I was holding back on him but not how much or exactly what, just that I wasn't telling it all.

At a bar down the street, The Gold Cage, Hump had a drink while I made a couple of calls. The first one was to The Man.

"I've been calling you everywhere," he said. He sounded mean and sleepy.

"We've been watching Atlanta's death rate go up. You got the call, huh?"

"Right after you left here."

"You stall?"

"As much as I could," The Man said. "Like you told me to I had him read off a page."

"And?" I turned and looked at the bar. Some hustler trim was talking to Hump.

"He seemed amused. He read me a page and he acted like he'd be glad to read the whole ledger to me."

Broken thumbs. Punishment for pushing the button a few too many times on a xerox machine? "How much of a stall?"

"Until Monday night. I told him I'd have to bring in the money from out of town."

"How and where?"

"He didn't say. He's careful. He'll call back here Monday evening early, he said."

That left me Sunday and a good part of Monday. It wasn't much.

"Hardman, I get the feeling I have made a mistake hiring you."

"Fire me. I need a Sunday off."

The hustler trim leaned against Hump and said something in his ear. Warm breath quoting the price. Five-oh for a lot of fun.

"It's too late. He wants you to make the delivery."

I said, "I'm close."

"That a firm promise?"

"No."

"Goddam it, Hardman."

"It's your fault. Who said you had to keep books as good as General Motors?"

After he called me a few names he hung up and I dialed Marcy's number.

"What are you doing?"

"Reggie and I are watching a movie. I think Audie Murphy is going to win in half an hour or so."

"Got anything to drink?"

"Remy Martin tempt you?"

"Hump and I'll be there for the final shoot-out."

Strong smell of coffee in the apartment. Marcy met me at the door and gave me a one-armed hug. Regina was seated on the sofa, dressed in dark slacks and a frilly white blouse. I said hello to her on the way past while I walked Marcy toward the kitchen. Hump stopped in the living room and I heard him say, "I'm sorry about your friend."

"We weren't that close," Regina said. "Of course, I'm sorry about…"

I lost the rest of it. Lost it in Marcy's breathing when I kissed her long and hard. "Everything all right here? She get moved in?"

"Yes to both questions."

I reached past her and got down the Remy Martin. The bottle was about two thirds full. I drew the cork and got down four glasses. After putting three of them aside I poured myself a stiff shot in the other one. "What do you think of her?"

"Kind of distant. I don't feel like I'm getting close to her."

"That might be a problem. She might think that's why I put her here."

"She'd think that?" Marcy was shocked.

"Could be." I lifted the glass and took a sip and rolled it around in my mouth. When I swallowed it hit my stomach like a red hot coal. "The kind of people she'd know, even when they play cards with their mother, they check the cards to make sure she didn't bring in a shaved deck."

"You the only one drinking around here?" Hump leaned a shoulder against the kitchen doorway.

"Not now that you've caught me." I tipped the bottle and poured shots for him and for Regina. Marcy got down cups and began to pour the coffee.

While Hump poured second shots, I got my topcoat and dug out the list of names I'd gotten from Heppler by way of his hard assed bodyguard. I passed the list to Regina. "Know any of these?"

It was dim light or it was too dim for her. She carried the list to the kitchen doorway. Standing there, back to us, while she read the names and addresses. The time it took her I figured she went through the list more than once.

"No." She turned back to us. "None of them. Are they supposed to?"

"Maybe not." I met her and took the list. "It was just a thought."

"Who are they?" She took her seat and lifted the cognac.

"People who played in the Wednesday games with Ronny."

"Oh." She sipped the cognac and made a little face at the burn from it.

"I thought you might have heard Ronny mention one or two of them."

"No, I don't think so. You know, he might have, but the names didn't mean anything to me at the time."

"Too bad." I folded the list and put it away. "It could have helped."

"How?" Regina asked.

I shrugged.

Hump leaned in. "It might have pared the list down for us."

"Well, since I don't know any of the five ..." Regina began.

Hump finished it for her. "Then we have to check all five out, from the ground up."

I picked up my empty cup. "More coffee in the pot?"

"About half a cup." Marcy led me into the kitchen. After she poured me the dregs she started past me. I shook my head at her and she edged around and moved close to me.

I leaned in and put my mouth close to her ear. "Anything happen here last night?" Last night? It seemed more like a week ago.

"Like what?"

"She leave? She make a phone call?"

"I don't know."

I read the hesitation. "Come on, Marcy. I didn't put her here so you'd have to inform on her, but I need to know."

"I can't be sure. I have a sort of half-awake memory. It must have been around midnight and I could hear her talking."

"In her sleep?"

"It might have been."

"But she slept on the sofa and the phone's in here." I gulped the coffee and got some sludge. "You ask her about it?"

"I wasn't sure I hadn't dreamed it and, if I hadn't it still didn't seem important."

I reached past her and placed the cup on the kitchen counter. "After we leave, you find out. Do it any way you can."

I took her hand and we joined Hump and Regina in the living room. Hump was telling her some wild-assed story about a week he and a couple of friends spent in Mexico City a few years ago. I'd heard the story about five times. He always seemed to tell it while I was still sober.

After Hump drove off I turned down my bed clothes and brushed my teeth. Before I stretched out, I got the list of five names and read it through a final time.

J. B. Stark
Suite 7, The Hudson House Annex

Whoever Stark was he was in the money. It was a fancy hotel with a special annex for people who lived there year around. I'd hate to have to pay his rent.

James Falco
5 Winston Place, N.E.

It took me some time to place the address. I was fairly certain it was one of those one-block lanes off Argonne. It was the section being taken over to some degree by the hippie element that was being run out of the tight squeeze area around the Strip. It wasn't the high rent district. I could mark hungry by his name.

Randy Bass
No. 22 Riveredge Apartments

Half one way, half the other. It was the kind of place that made a bit of a thing about singles activity. Advertised in the Sunday paper with pictures of girls in brief bathing suits lounging around a pool. Probably for the young single executive who liked to drink and party and get laid on a regular basis. It might mean that Randy wasn't a full-time nightcrawler. A question mark by him.

Dusty Roads or Rhodes
344 Dogwood Lane
Decatur

I'd never known anybody with the last name Roads or Rhodes who didn't get nicknamed Dusty. Even girls. I wasn't sure about Dogwood Lane. Out in Decatur there was a wide range, from low rent to $150,000 homes and all the steps in between. It was a waste of time trying to figure this one in economic terms.

Conway Burris
Elgin Hotel

It was an easy one. The far extreme from the Hudson House. The Elgin was pure fly-by-night. It was a short money place. Where you lived on the way up or the way down, if you were a gambler or some other kind of hustler. Back in the 1920's it was a respectable family hotel. A visitor to Atlanta might stay there with his wife and kids. Not anymore. He'd get mugged on the way from his room to the creaky elevator. So Burris rated a star rather than a question mark.

Screw the list. I put it under the alarm clock after I set the alarm for eight o'clock.

It was dark in the room. I thought the alarm had gone off. I kept fumbling at the back of the clock, trying to push in the switch, but it was already in and the ringing went on and on. So I dropped the clock on the bed next to me and lifted the telephone receiver.

It was Marcy. "She's gone."

"Who? What?"

"Regina's gone."

"Went out for breakfast," I said.

"All her things are gone."

I kicked the covers away and sat up. "She leave a note?"

"Nothing."

"You ask her about that call you thought you heard her make?"

"Yes. She said she was calling the man who lived in the apartment next to hers, the one she had on Briarcliff."

I dug back for the name. "Bob something. Harris, I think."

"I guess that's it."

"When did she leave?"

"I don't know. Whenever it was, she was awful quiet about it."

I felt around the bed covers until I found the clock. Seven-ten. "She say why she called Harris?"

"To see if there was any mail there for her."

I stared at the clock again. It still showed seven-ten. "You always wake up this early?"

"The cognac gave me a stomach burn. I went to the kitchen to *get* a glass of milk and I found she'd—"

"Go back to bed, Marcy. I'll call you later."

"Bye."

I found the Atlanta white pages under the bed. Cotton candy dust floated out with it. I blew that away and plopped the book on the bed. I found a Robert Harris on Briarcliff. I couldn't remember the number over there but the one listed for him seemed close enough, in the right part of the street. I dialed the number and let it ring. It rang for about two minutes before he answered it.

"Yeah? What the fuck—?"

"Police," I said. "This is Wilson."

"Oh." I could almost feel the strain of Harris trying to pull the parts of his head back together. "Look, if it's about that noise last night—?"

"It's not. It's about the girl who lived next door to you for a couple of months."

"Sure," he said. "Regina Clark."

"She moved out last Monday, right?"

"Yeah."

"The Friday before that you had tickets to a Hawks game. You dropped by somewhere around eight-thirty or so and invited her to the game."

"No, you've got it mixed up. It wasn't that Friday. It was a week before that. Maybe two weeks before that."

Check and double check. "You hear from her since she moved out?"

"Not a peep," he said.

"No phone call from her a couple of nights before?"

"No."

"No call to see if she'd received any mail?"

"No. Like I said not a peep. Look, is she in any trouble?"

"Thanks for your help, Mr. Harris."

"About that noise last night—"

I hung up on him.

Before I went in to shower, I pulled the curtains aside and had a look at the weather outside. Cold and gray, a bad day to try to recoup a screw-up. If any day ever was. If any day ever wasn't.

I stayed under the shower until my eyeballs fogged.

CHAPTER EIGHT

All down the hallway the Sunday editions of the *Journal-Constitution* were stacked in front of the doors. Here and there, placed on top of the local papers, an early edition of the *New York Times*. Oh, that is status in the South. People who lived in the annex to the Hudson House could afford it.

No *Times* in front of No. 7. I bent over and picked up the couple of pounds of *Journal-Constitution* and nodded at Hump. He reached past me and gave the buzzer a push. I counted up to about sixty and nodded again. Hump gave it a longer ride this time.

I didn't so much hear the angry stomping as I felt it. It was barefooted, without the hard edges, and it stopped on the other side of the door.

"Who is it?"

"Jim Hardman."

"Who?"

"Heppler sent me."

The door swung open. "What does Mort want this time of day?"

I looked down the hall. "We come in? I don't like talking in halls."

He waved us in. I looked around for a place to unload the paper. He dipped his head toward an easy chair next to a brocaded sofa. The apartment, what I could see of it, had that temporary look. He'd spent a bit of money furnishing it but not more than half an hour trying to decide how he wanted it to look.

From a slightly cracked door to the right, a girl asked, "Who is it, Harry?"

"It's not your daddy," he yelled back. He looked at me and let his eyes brush across Hump. "That dumb cunt thinks my name is Harry."

Stark wasn't more than about five-three. Wide blocky shoulders and a chest like a tree trunk. I put his age at about forty-two or three. A peppering of gray along his temples, a coarse-skinned face, maybe Greek.

"What does Mort want?"

"He didn't call you?"

"Was he supposed to?"

I'd thought he'd delayed so he could ask around. So he could get permission. "I thought he would."

"Get on with it," he said.

"We're poking around in Ronny's murder."

"Cops?" His laugh didn't have a speck of humor in it. "I let cops in my house?"

"Not cops," I said.

"That's better." But he still had the wary look.

"The Friday Ronny was killed we think he might have been playing cards with some people at his place. He ask you?"

Stark looked around the living room. It was a slow, unhurried look. He located a pack of cigarettes and walked over and shook one out. He lit it and coughed. "Let me tell you something about myself."

"All right."

"When I was a kid, I was a dumb kid. What do you expect from a kid who comes over on a boat and can't even speak the language? But I learned fast. I took the crash course. I learned to speak the language and everything else I needed to know. The last thirty years or so I haven't done one dumb thing. You got that?" I nodded. "Knowing that, you think I'm going to waste an evening playing penny, nickel and dime with Ronny?"

"You knew he was flat?"

"Flat? No, just chicken. He didn't have the nerve to bet what he had."

"But you played with him on Wednesdays."

"He was Mort's friend. Mort can do social work if he wants to."

"Social work?"

"You know, trying to pump him up, trying to give him his nerve back." Another puff at the cigarette and another cough. "And it won't work. You play cards, you play the same way for a dollar that you do for a thousand. You don't shift gears between Wednesday and Friday."

"Harry?" It was the girl calling from the bedroom.

"Yeah?"

"Bring me some juice when you come."

"Sure, baby."

"The others who played on Wednesdays, you know which ones might have played with Ronny on a Friday?"

"Any of them. All of them. How the shit should I know?"

He led us to the door and swung it open. "Sorry to hear about Ronny. That was a hard way to go."

I stopped in the doorway. "Twenty years ago he was the match of anybody in town."

Dull hard eyes looking out at me. "I wasn't in town then."

The Elgin Hotel hadn't changed. The smell of dust, of rusty steam heat and garbage blew down the halls in waves. Several of the tenants had put their trash cans outside their doors to be emptied by the hotel help. The help hadn't made the rounds yet. Just walking by I could see chicken bones, sandwich wrappers, outside edges of pizza crusts.

We were on the third floor outside of room 303. Hump knocked. No answer. He tried the door. It wasn't locked. That was foolishness at the Elgin. I'd known people to get killed for a couple of dollars or over a bottle of booze.

We went on in. Conway Burris was stretched out on the narrow bed. He was face down, wearing a dingy gray t-shirt and ragged red silk shorts. The smell of something sour like vomit was in the room. Hump walked around the bed and looked down at him. I passed up the look and gave the top of the dresser a look through. A five and a couple of singles, a bowl of change. Four unbroken decks of cards and next to them a catalog from the Windy City Gaming Company. I flipped through the catalog. There was a bit of wordage in there about doing card tricks on your friends but the main product offered for sale was the line of marked cards, *readers,* cards with minor changes in the designs on the backs. Across the table you could read the values of the high cards in the deck. The catalog gave me the idea that the four decks of sealed cards were probably marked.

I circled the bed and looked down at Burris. Head and face almost buried under his shoulder. A couple of days of stubble on his face. Hair thinning. Old before his time. On the floor beside the bed an empty pint gin bottle. Next to the bottle a drying sticky stain that might have been vomit the evening before.

I shook my head at Hump and we backed out of the room. Out in the hall, the door closed behind us. Hump said, "Not sure that stud could tell us much."

I nodded.

"He's not the master criminal type."

"Hardly." We stopped at the elevator. "Fifty thousand paid and another hundred on the way and he's learning to play readers? Not a chance."

Two down and three to go.

The Riveredge Apartments and not a river in sight in any direction. Hastily built junk apartments. When the spring came grass would probably grow up between the tiles in the living rooms.

We'd been on the narrow porch for a few minutes. I'd tried the bell. No answer. I gave up on that and began to bang the doorframe with the fat bottom of my fist.

"Hey. Hey, you." It was a woman's voice from the next door apartment.

"Yeah?"

"Randy's not here."

I stepped off the side of the porch and walked over to the woman's apartment. I didn't go up onto the porch. I stood on the walk and looked up at her. A hard, young face with frizzled red hair. It might have been a mod hairdo but I didn't think so.

"Where is he?"

"He left town."

"When?"

"Almost three weeks ago. His company transferred him to Denver."

"What company?"

"Beneficial Mutual."

"Thanks."

"Don't thank me," the girl said. "Anything to keep you from knocking the fucking building down."

Her door closed with a squeak.

Two left on the list.

I'd made a good guess the night before. Winston is one of those short blocks off Argonne. A man with good wind could spit from one end to the other. I counted four houses and the rest were empty lots, some with "For Sale" signs out in the winter brush stubble.

No. 5 looked like a doll's house for rich kids. Flat and only one floor. A screened-in porch off to the left. The main entrance to the right. The front lawn a mess. Like mine, the fall leaves hadn't been raked away.

The Sunday paper on the steps. A rutted driveway, without a car in it, pushed up past the house. White paint was blistered and chipping on the front door. No answer after a few times. I rubbed the cold, sore knuckles and stepped off the cinderblock stoop. Hump led the way around the back. Watching our steps in the mud ruts.

It was a small backyard. A rusting barbecue grill was next to the back steps. A thin layer of ice was on the water in the grill, a red ice.

I stuffed my hands in my pockets and let Hump do the knocking this time. Another couple of minutes and there still wasn't any sign of life in the house.

"Can you spring the lock, Hump?"

"Think so."

I looked around. There was an empty lot off to the left and a wintered-in backyard on the right. No sign of anybody in the yard or watching from the windows. "Go ahead."

Hump leaned his shoulder against the door. He gripped the knob. He bumped the door a couple of times with all his weight. I heard the lock fall apart on the other side of the door.

Waiting. No sound inside. He pushed the door in and it hit the remainder of the lock. It skidded across the floor. We were in the kitchen. No light burned there. Passing the stove, I looked down at the skillet. Five or six fish sticks, fried dark and hard, in a thick white grease. I tried the refrigerator. Five cans of Drewry's beer. A part of a half gallon of milk, soured. Half a loaf of bread, some French's mustard and a pack of pickle and olive loaf.

The living room was beyond. There was a battered green sofa and a coffee table and a dark blue carpet worn thin at the entrance to the kitchen and across the way at the front door.

The bedroom was off to the left. Past that a light burned in the bathroom. The bed had been slept in. I touched the sheets and found there was a gritty feel, like they hadn't been changed for a couple of weeks. Hump passed me on the way into the bathroom. I went back to the wall next to the bedroom entrance and flipped on the lights. I crossed to the closet. Clothing still hung there. I squatted and looked in the bottom part of the closet. There it was. A clean spot surrounded by dust. A suitcase had been there. A large suitcase.

Hump came from the bathroom. He held out a tube of something. "That mushmouth sound the man has."

"Yeah?"

"Orafix."

"That's thin," I said. "You know how many people have dentures?"

"Add this." From behind his back he held out a bottle of perfume.

I read the label. Straw Hat. "So what?"

He dropped the tube of denture adhesive on the bed and uncapped the perfume. I got a whiff of it. It was familiar but ...

"Regina wears this."

"So do a lot of other women in the world." Orafix and Straw Hat. It wasn't enough.

I left him in the bedroom and looked around in the living room. I found a few paperback novels, some back issues of *Time* and the first issue of a magazine called *Gambler's World*. In the drawer under the coffee table I uncovered a handful of grass butts. Saved and not to be used until the supply ran out.

"Jim?"

I walked over and stood in the doorway.

"This Falco guy is a packrat. Can't throw anything away." He was digging around in the top drawer of the dresser.

"Like what?"

"Las Vegas memories." He held up a handful of book matches. "The Sands, the Golden Nugget, places like that." He held up a thin booklet in a plastic holder. "Savings book from a Vegas bank. Left ten dollars in it."

"It's not enough." I edged in and started digging around in one end of the packed drawer. Letters, old check stubs, scraps of paper with names and phone numbers written on them, blurring and drying out, ready to vanish like they'd been written with magic ink. I found a brass hash pipe, the screen in the bowl hardly discolored.

"Try this," Hump said.

It was a black and white polaroid picture. Turning brown now. A naked girl standing at a window. Her back is to the camera but her face is turned to the camera, as if she'd been called the split second before the picture was taken. The face is in three-quarters profile, a smiling sensual thrust above her shoulder. Below the arm, there because she had twisted her body slightly, is the outline of a tight small breast that would just fit into the palm of a hand.

"Regina?" Hump asked.

"Yes, that's the bitch."

The two strings are knotted. The hustler girl from Las Vegas and the question mark named James Falco.

"Run the tape for me."

The Man scooted his chair around and punched the "Play" button.

"See how dependable I am? I said I'd call back and I did."

"It wouldn't hurt my feelings if you got lost," The Man said.

"I plan to. As soon as I get my hands on the hundred thousand."

"I'm not sure I can trust you," The Man said. *"I thought it was a one-time pay-off and here you are at the trough again."*

"*That's the way I am. Piggy, piggy.*"

"*You've got the copy of the ledger there?*"

Crackling of paper. "*Right in front of me.*"

"*Read me page 4 and page 31.*"

A laugh, a wet sputter. "*Now you're getting cute.*"

"*If you've got it read it.*"

"*The fact that you ask interests me. I suppose there's some good reason?*"

"*Suppose what you want to.*"

"*Page 4?*" Mushmouth began to read the column of figures. "Skip that," I said.

The Man ran the tape forward and punched the "Play" button once more. Mushmouth was still reading figures. "This is almost the end of it," The Man said.

"You said the call came right after we left last night?"

"I checked my watch." The Man selected one of his special blend cigarettes from a box and lit it. "It was eight-fifteen."

I circled the table and hit the "Stop" button. "We fingered Tony Mitchell without meaning to."

Hump's head jerked back. He'd had his head down, listening to the reading of hundreds and thousands. "You sure, Jim?"

"Somewhere on the other side of seventy percent," I said. "Something happened to make Mushmouth or Falco or whoever think Mitchell had done a tricky to him. He got the idea that Mitchell might have a copy of the ledger. Friday night he has a question and answer session with Mitchell. Maybe Mitchell convinces him it's not true, but Mushmouth breaks his thumbs anyway. Why his thumbs? Probably because thumbs press copy machine buttons."

The Man said, "I don't see how we fingered Mitchell."

"Sure you do. He calls you at eight-fifteen. But, the way I told you to, you're playing it cozy. You ask him to read a couple of pages. You ask him to prove he's got a copy."

Hump nodded. "It starts him thinking and what he comes up with is Mitchell."

"Maybe he doesn't know what Mitchell's done. He might even guess that Mitchell has called you himself and made a demand. What he does know is that Mitchell lied to him."

"Bang," Hump said.

"Actually," I said, "it was two bangs." I leaned over the tape recorder and hit the "Play" button.

Mushmouth said, *"That match what you've got?"*

"It matches."

"You got the money?"

"I've got to bring it in from out of town. It ought to be here late Monday morning or early in the afternoon."

"The same bagman. I want Hardman."

"He's got some doubts."

"Screw his doubts."

"Why does it have to be him? There ought to be ten other—"

"Because he's fat and dumb and slow and he's got a cute ass on him." A laugh. *"And he needs the money for his old age."*

"I'll talk to him."

"Do more than that. Convince him."

"When and where?" The Man said.

"I'll call you. Early Monday evening."

"That's it," The Man said. I punched the "Stop" button.

"I need something else from Vegas. You pay off that security man out there yet?"

"He's been paid."

"Have him check out James Falco. Must have spent some time out there. Might have been a gambler. Might have been a house dealer."

"I'll call him right now."

"I'll need it as soon as you get it."

"I'll offer top dollar."

One of The Man's soldiers drifted in from the other room. He went to the refrigerator and took out a platter with about a pound of lox on it, a huge block of cream cheese and a bowl of kosher dills. From another shelf he lifted down a whole loaf of sour rye.

"Have a snack," The Man said.

I shook my head. "No chitterlings?"

"Not where I live. Those things stink."

That was true enough.

At my place Hump turned on the TV. The first game of the Sunday pro football doubleheader was almost over. I closed out the sound by shutting the bedroom door.

Art's wife, Edna, answered the phone. "Jim, when are you coming by to see us?"

"Soon as I can."

"You never have time for us."

"I've been busy. Is Art up yet?"

"He's in the shower."

I said I'd call back.

"No, here he is. He fooled me."

Art said, "Don't you rest on Sunday like everybody else?"

"When I can. Look, Regina Clark bugged out on us."

"Tell me about it."

I did. At the end he said, "I meant to check out her story, where she was supposed to be the night Ronny was killed. I just never got to it."

"I've got a new name for you. James Falco, 5 Winston Place. But don't bother to look for him there. He's gone too. I think Regina Clark got there before I did and warned him off."

"What do you want out of me?"

"His record, if he's got one. A photo."

"It's Sunday," Art said, "and I'm doing your scut work again."

"Or I've been doing yours."

❀ ❀ ❀

The second game was from the west coast, the 49-ers and the Lions. It was halftime when I heard the car out in the driveway. I went to the kitchen and got a Bud and handed it to Art as soon as he cleared the door. Art shucked his topcoat and sat down facing the TV.

"About time you got color," he said.

"The next big score."

"That Falco's a strange one."

"Found him, huh?"

"He's a local boy. Raised here. Nothing on him but some juvenile and the court sealed that. The way I heard it it was small time breaking and entering at 16 and 17."

It didn't sound right. Extortion and murder were things you went to school to learn.

"So I went national and checked him out. Three arrests, one for pandering, one for armed robbery, one for dealing in funny money."

"Can't decide on a major?"

"One conviction. He did four on the armed robbery."

"A photo?"

"One's on the way. Got a bit of the skinny on him ahead of time." He brought a pad out of his pocket. "He's twenty-eight, six-one, about one-ninety. Dark hair. Girls like him and think he's handsome. Word is he hustles them good when he's short. No complaints from the women. Must give good value for money received."

"What else?"

"A tattoo on his right bicep. 'Born To Win' on the background of a twenty dollar bill. A scar on his chin." He put the pad away. "Word is the scar goes back to his pimping days. A girl went after him with a beer can opener. That was before pop tops."

The scar reminded me of something. It was close and I almost had it before it floated away.

Art sipped the Bud. "You telling me everything, Jim?"

"Most of it."

"What's left out?"

"The part I didn't tell you."

"Smartass." He claw-fingered at my shirt pocket and got one of my smokes. "If Ronny was flat, why would Falco and the girl *go* after him?"

"Maybe they didn't know it." I lit the smoke for him. "What the girl knew about Ronny went back to Vegas. She saw him as a high roller. Must have thought he had a stash."

"And the Winters girl?" He blew smoke at me. "Where did she fit in?"

"I don't know."

"Tony Mitchell?"

"I think he was in it with them."

"Why was he killed?"

"I don't know."

"That's all I get around here."

"Except for free beer and free cigarettes."

Art stood up. He tilted back his head and poured the rest of the beer down. He put on his topcoat.

"Don't rush off. Stay for the second half."

"I'll come back when you've got color," he said.

"You got color at home?"

"Me? With four kids to support?" He gave me a sour grunt and headed for the door.

Later in the evening, while Marcy and I were watching the Sunday Night Movie, a police cruiser dropped off a sealed envelope. It contained a full face and profile of James Falco.

One look at the photos and it made sense. The memory of the scar drifted by again and I grabbed at it. I knew where I'd seen him that one time before. It had been at the dance studio the afternoon we located Regina Clark. He'd been with her in the dance instruction room and they'd led me to believe that Falco was a student. Played a scene for me and foxed me good, those two.

All the ifs and therefores rattled around in my head.

If I'd thought to check the studio log, I'd have realized that Regina didn't have an appointment for the time period we'd spent in the reception room. If I'd known that, I could have made my guess why Betty Winters had to be killed. Betty Winters knew who Falco was. If, during the time she spent with Hump, the Winters girl talked, we'd check Falco out and the whole mess might split open.

Therefore Regina had called Falco from Marcy's apartment that night. Therefore Falco had probably gone to the Winters girl's apartment and waited out in the hall until she opened the door. If you can do one killing you can do two. And three is as easy as two.

I got sick of the ifs and therefores and stuffed the photos back in the envelope. I went into the kitchen and mixed myself a fistful of J&B.

CHAPTER NINE

M onday morning was sunny and cold.

Hump took one of the pictures of Regina Clark and the full face shot of Falco and spent the morning and the early afternoon flashing them around the downtown transient hotels. I did a trip back into the past. The days on the force I'd known some informers. Now I traced five of them. One was in the slam for beating his wife, another had died of an overdose six months ago and the other three acted like they didn't know me now.

After lunch, I did a loop around the city, trying to touch as many of the perimeter motels as I could. It was nothing and double nothing. At four, I packed it in and drove home. I'd showered and changed clothes and cleaned and reloaded the .38 P.P. when Hump dropped by.

A shake of his head and I knew he'd drawn an egg too. Not that I'd expected much from it. It was time fill, a one in a thousand chance that we'd find a string. But it was harder sitting around and waiting for the dark. The dark had a lot of trouble in it. I couldn't back out now but I had second thoughts and third thoughts about it. And my stomach felt like somebody'd been throwing their old lighted cigarette butts down my throat.

At five-thirty, it was time to leave for The Man's apartment. I'd locked the front door and hit the top step on my way down when Art drove his unmarked car past my driveway and parked out on the street. While he got out and headed for the lawn, Hump gave me a questioning look.

"Meet you there," I said.

I waited in the leaf clutter of the lawn, the wet rot that went back to the fall leaf drop. Art stopped a few feet from me and looked over his shoulder at Hump. Hump waved and Art waved back.

"Something going on?"

"The usual. We split the town down the middle. Falco and the girl have to be somewhere."

"Why?"

"Huh?"

"Either you know something you haven't told me or you've gone dummy on me. If I was Falco or the girl I'd be a thousand miles from here and still going."

Hump backed down the drive. I watched him. I needed the time to think. What Art said was true enough. Without the hundred thousand to anchor them in town, they'd have been pushing west or toward Mexico. But I couldn't tell Art about the hundred thousand so I'd have to run my mouth a bit and hope I found something to say sooner or later.

"Falco's too smart," I said.

"What's that supposed to mean?"

"He knows how we think. He knows we've been looking for him since yesterday. He knows step two is to widen the search area. That's why he's in Atlanta. He's found himself a hole and pulled the shadows in over him."

Art said, "Something stinks." His hard, narrowed eyes looked out at me from the flat Irish face.

"It's that goddam fig tree. It smells like cat piss."

"Don't play games with me, Jim."

"Huh?"

"You know they're still in town and you've got a card you're not showing me." Art blew his cloudy breath at me. "We got to stand out here in the yard and freeze?"

"I'm late getting somewhere."

"Really? Well, I've got an hour to waste. We go in my car or yours?"

"Not today," I said. "Later in the week let's get together and ride around and yell nasty things at girls."

"Got a smoke?"

I reached in the yoke of the topcoat. Art stepped in closer and held out his right hand. I was bringing the cigarette pack out when he slapped his left hand against my right topcoat pocket. The .38 banged hard against my thigh and there was a dull clatter from the handful of spare shells.

"You still want the smoke?" I edged around until the right side was away from him.

"I was right. Something's going down tonight."

I shook the pack at him until one smoke popped out. "Nothing's going down unless we have luck. You'll be the first one I call."

He took the smoke and lit it. "I could bust you right here on the spot."

"Do it. Tonight might be shitty anyway."

He blew a curl of smoke at me. "Why are you carrying?"

"Because I wasn't Saturday night."

"You've got a better reason than that."

"Tell me what it is," I retorted.

Art's got a temper. I could feel the rough edges of it. "You're making this hard, Jim."

"That's the way it is. Kiss me or leave me alone." I walked past him and opened the car door. I left the door open while I started the engine and let it warm up a bit.

Art followed me and said, "I could dog you all night."

"It's your time. Waste it."

I closed the door and backed down the drive. When I reached the road, he was still there, head down, digging his toe into the dirt. A couple of blocks from the house, I looked back and he was tailgating me. He remained there for five or six blocks. Then, when I caught a light, he pulled up level, in the lane for a left turn. I looked over at him. He gave me the high finger.

The light changed. I headed straight on and he took a slow wide left.

❧   ❧   ❧

"I thought you'd found better things to do," Hump said.

"I considered it." I watched the black with the pumpgun. He placed my .38 on the bar counter before he ducked under the far end and placed a snifter on the bar. I said, "A short one." He poured me about an ounce of the Hines. I took it and walked over and stood looking down at Hump. He was sprawled on the white sofa. "Anything yet?"

"Nothing." He nodded at a place next to him on the sofa. "What's with Art?"

"He thinks we didn't invite him to the party because he still has pimples."

"Not enough girls to go around as it is." He tilted his head toward the bedroom door. "Only one girl here and The Man's got her."

"Nice?"

"New girl from out of town," Hump said.

"Auditioning?"

"Oh, shit, yes." Hump put his head back and closed his eyes, a smile on his face.

Exactly at seven the phone rang.

The bodyguard answered it. I couldn't hear what he mumbled into the phone. He passed us on the way to the bedroom door. He knocked once on the door, the discreet rap butlers make in English movies. A minute later The Man came out. He was wearing slacks, bedroom slippers and a red velvet smoking jacket.

"You got here after all?" he said.

"Thought I might as well." I stood up and followed him into the kitchen-dining room. I looked back and saw Hump lean and look into the bedroom before the black bodyguard closed the door.

The Man lifted the receiver. "Yes?"

The tape recorder was running. It had developed a squeak, like the tapehead needed some work.

Hump walked in, some spring in his step, and sat down at the table. I leaned toward him. "Prime?" He grinned and nodded.

"For you," The Man said.

I took the receiver. "Hardman, here."

"You got the cash?" The mushmouth sound was gone. He was wearing his teeth or the bridge. The accent was southern, but flattened out some by time in other places.

"It's ready now."

"You've been making some guesses," he said.

"A few." I decided I might as well hang some of it out on the line. It might be worth my life later. He might kill if he thought he could protect his identity. If he knew it wouldn't do any good, maybe he'd settle for the hundred thousand. "The girl gave some of it away."

"What girl?"

"The Clark girl. The afternoon at the dance studio when she talked to me and the cop she got rattled. She thought we'd boxed her in and she made up a lie to throw us off. Said there was supposed to be a poker game that night at Ronny's. That was to get us running in circles. It did at first. Later on, it put me on to you. That and some other lies."

"Good help is hard to find," he said.

"That's true enough, Falco. Where's the drop to be?"

"Same place. In front of the Omni."

"At the stairwell?"

"At the curb. You'll get your instructions there."

"When?"

"Eight on the dot. Come alone and no iron."

"All right."

The Man leaned past me and grabbed the receiver. I backed away. The Man said, "You. You, Falco, this is the last payday. No more copies and no more phone calls."

I left the kitchen-dining room and slumped down on the sofa. Hump came after me and leaned an elbow on the bar. "On tonight?"

"At eight."

"You need me?"

I nodded. "You're the lead-tag."

The phone got slammed down in the back of the apartment. Seconds later The Man stormed in and stood in the center of the living room with a clenched fist on his hip. "That one is dead. His hide is on the wall."

"One thing," I said. "When I make the swap, I don't want your boys shucking and jiving around me. You want Falco you do it on your own time, after I'm back home in my bed."

He didn't want to agree to it. I could feel the hard breath he was holding back. I matched eyeballs with him and waited. I had all night and he knew it. When it came, I had to lean toward him to hear it. "If that's the way you want it."

"I'll make you a promise. I see any of your boys tagging me and I'll turn around and bring the money back here. I see any of them at the Omni and I might make a mistake and shoot one."

The black bodyguard looked at me and looked away.

"All right, Hardman." He banged the fist against his thigh. "But I want something for my money. I want that copy and I want to be sure it's the last copy."

"I think it's a straight swap this time. A one for one. No reason to do it otherwise. He's overstayed himself. He'll take the money and run." I found my glass and tossed down the last swallow of Hines. "If Falco was really smart, he'd have taken the fifty thousand, written off the rest, and headed for the high grass."

Hump said, "That's the way I read it. He's taking a risk tonight that he won't take again."

I placed the snifter on the bar. "Where's the money?"

The bodyguard leaned over the bar and brought up a Samsonite briefcase. After he placed it on the bar, I flipped the catches and ruffled the stacks of tens and twenties. I stepped away. The bodyguard closed the briefcase and pressed the catches.

"Got an evening paper?"

"Why?" The Man looked puzzled.

"In the kitchen," the bodyguard said.

"Just the sports page," I called after him.

He brought it to me. It was opened to the right section. I found what I'd been looking for on the second page. It was a small block with a heavy black border.

I passed the paper to Hump. Hump looked up from it. "That's either smart or dumb."

"Let's hope it's dumb." I put on my topcoat and dropped the .38 in the right hand pocket. I picked up the briefcase. "Wish us luck," I said to The Man.

He didn't say anything. His eyes were on the briefcase all the way out the door, until the slope of the stairs dropped us out of sight.

Out in the cold wind, Hump stood by while I unlocked the trunk of my car and tossed the briefcase inside. He slammed the lid shut and then we sat in my car and smoked a slow one while I explained the lead-tag and how I wanted it to work.

We leapfrogged back downtown to North Avenue. Past the Varsity and a left onto Techwood. All that loop around was so we'd approach the Omni on the right side of the drive, the curb side instead of the parking lot one. The traffic was already bumper to bumper and I got some drivers mad by holding up the flow to let Hump move into a slot right ahead of me. From there on it was Hump's job to jockey about and move up one car so he wouldn't be directly in front of me.

It was about a mile from North Avenue and Techwood to the Omni. The last half mile was slow going. It was that southern gentleman crap. Drivers dropping their wives and girlfriends off in front of the sports complex and then heading for the parking lots. All that so those delicate ladies wouldn't get chilled.

By five of eight, I was still a hundred yards away. It was stop and go. We'd shaved it close. Hump was two cars ahead, also in the curb lane. Off at about thirty degrees to the right I could see the flare of lights from the Omni. All that glass and the red rusting steel in a kind of desert.

Fifty yards away. I got the piece out of my coat. I placed it on the seat next to me and looked around for an obvious and handy stash. Not under the seat. Too hard to reach when I needed it. Not in the glove box. That had the same problems.

I settled on the litter basket on the floorboards between the driver and the passenger seat. It was the kind that had the heavy rubber flaps that anchor it. I pushed the trash forward and made an opening. I stuffed the .38 in and scattered cigarette packs and a waxed sandwich wrapper over it. Have to think ahead. I got out my pack of smokes. Half a pack left. I shook all of them out and put one back in. I stored the rest of them in the glove box. I tossed the pack on the dashboard next to a book of matches.

Ready now? Not quite. I remembered the half a dozen spare shells. I scooped them out and dropped them in my left trouser pocket with my change. Now I was ready.

The line of cars moved. Almost there. Hump was level with the Omni now and edging forward. The blue Mustang between us didn't take much time unloading. Two young girls and a guy got out and hurried away, out of the wind. The Mustang whipped around Hump and headed for the ground-level lot. I edged up to fill the spot right behind Hump.

It wouldn't be long before the contact. It couldn't be. Already the cars stacked behind me were hitting their horns. All around me people were streaming into the Omni. The Hawks don't draw as well as the Flames but 8,000 is a fairly good crowd.

More honking behind me. A stationwagon on my tailgate unloaded a woman and a couple of boys and whipped around me.

A ribbon of people crossing ahead of me on a crosswalk.

Hands on the curbside doors at the same time. A blast of cold air hit me from the side and the back. James Falco slipped into the seat next to me. I caught a blur in the rearview mirror. It was a woman's face with a dark scarf over her hair. The doors closed. I could smell her perfume. Straw Hat. It was Regina Clark.

Falco brought out a .38 with a two-inch barrel and placed it across his leg. "Drive, Hardman."

Ahead of me Hump pulled away from the curb. I gave him a beat of about five and followed. Half a block away from the Omni Falco said, "Take a look."

Regina Clark twisted around and propped her elbows on the back of the rear seat. She stared out at the drive behind us for half a minute or so. "Nothing," she said.

CHAPTER TEN

Careful now. I kept my distance from Hump's car. Had to make sure that Falco didn't make a connection between his car and mine. Had to keep him, instead, thinking of the empty drive behind us. No, not empty now. One set of headlights about a block behind. Doing it easy, casually, I reached up and adjusted the rearview mirror. Falco edged around and looked through the back window.

"Car back there," Falco said. "Keep an eye on it."

And that was fine. Let him watch that while I remained a hundred yards behind Hump. Close enough so that I could let Hump know when Falco ordered me one way or the other. Either by signal lights or by changing lanes.

"He turned off," Regina said.

Falco said, "Is there a suitcase back there?"

After some moments of feeling around, Regina said, "I can't find it."

"Where is it, Hardman?"

"Where's the copy?"

"Regina's got it," Falco said.

"Let me see it."

A few seconds later, Regina passed the thick chunk of xerox pages over the seat back to Falco. The wide sheets were folded once and held in place by heavy twine. Falco showed it to me and dropped it on the seat between us.

"Now, where's the cash?"

"In the trunk."

"Goddam it, why the trunk?"

"Until I saw the copy, it was no trade. That's the way The Man wanted it."

"Screw him."

Heading toward Marietta Street. "Where are we going?"

"Don't be in a hurry. You might not like it." He grinned at me, showing the regular uppers with the browning crooked lowers. So it *was* probably a bridge. "Take a left on Marietta."

I hit my blinkers and moved into the turn lane. Ahead of me, without seeming to force it, Hump did the same. I slowed a bit and he speeded up. By the time the turn came, he'd widened the gap.

"Check," Falco said.

"Nothing."

"That's good." Falco relaxed. "Hang a left on Peachtree."

We caught the red light on Forsyth. I didn't see Hump anywhere.

"Put your gun on his neck," Falco said.

A touch of cold metal on my neck, between the cords. I sat still, hands on the wheel, while Falco ran his hands over me. Shoulders and armpits, back, waist, my legs down to my shoe tops and even across my crotch.

Falco leaned away from me. "All right." The short-barrel .38 easy on his leg again.

I got the green light and moved off. We were in the cruising section now, the area where the black pimps tooled around in their high wheel cars with the white fake fur seat covers. One of those in front of me and one behind. I hoped Hump was awake out there somewhere.

I took the turn on Peachtree and headed back toward the center of town. We were making a kind of box step, a wide runaround, while Falco satisfied himself that we didn't have a tag. "Where now, Falco?"

"Aren't you an eager one?"

"You can sit on my lap and drive if you'd rather," I said.

"To the Strip."

"Noisy down there this time of night."

"That's right."

"And one more bit of noise won't matter, huh?" I thought I could read him. He had a burn on against me and sometime in the last day or so he'd made out his own death contract on me. Just because I balled up a good score he had going. Just because I tracked the blood to him and wrote his name in the blood puddle.

"Maybe you're not as dumb as I thought," he said.

Regina put her hands on the seat back and leaned between us. "You said there wouldn't be any more killing."

"Who said anything about killing?"

That flattened out in the air around us. Regina Clark lifted her hands and backed away. "It sounded that way," she said.

"Watch the back window and shut up," he said.

Approaching Baker, I took the curb lane in front of the Regency and followed the northeast part of the Peachtree Street split. It didn't seem to bother him. So maybe we were going as far as the Strip, the area around 10th Street.

Passing 3rd Street Falco said, "You're in no hurry, are you?"

"No reason why I should be." Bowels in an uproar. I needed to piss. A sickness in my stomach. Where the hell was Hump anyway?

"You know the Follies?"

I did. It was one of those expense account lunch and dinner places where all the waitresses were just about topless and gave you a thick serving of titty along with your prime rib. It was set back from the street, behind the Radio Shack on 8th and Peachtree.

"Turn in there."

Nothing else I could do. I passed 8th and swung up the drive that cut into the sidewalk. A number of empty spaces were there.

"To the back of the lot and to the left," Falco said.

It was dark back there, the long shadow of the building covering about half the lot. It looked like a mugger's paradise. Maybe for that reason there weren't a lot of cars back there.

"That space against the building," Falco said.

I pulled in and braked. Falco reached across me and turned the ignition off and withdrew the keys. "Regina."

He didn't have to tell her what to do. I felt the cold iron touch the cord on one side on my neck. He reached behind him and grabbed the door handle.

"Mind if I smoke?"

It amused him. "Go ahead. It happens in all the best movies."

"The last smoke?" I got the Pall Mall pack from the dash and found the book of matches. I made a thing of trying to shake the one smoke out, at the same time pinching the pack so it wouldn't. Finally I tore the rest of the top off and picked out the single cigarette.

"That's funny," Falco said. "Just one left and it's all you're going to need."

I waited while he opened the door and got out. Waited until he closed the door and cut the overhead light. Then I lipped the smoke and lit it. Hand up so that she could see it, I crushed the Pall Mall pack and shoved my hand down into the litter basket. I got the butt of the .38 the first time. I drew it up in one movement and placed it in my lap. A short beat and the hand continued upward to take the cigarette from my mouth as I blew a thin stream of smoke toward the roof of the car.

Outside, the top of the trunk swung up and blocked the back window. I dropped my left hand and caught the .38, found the safety and clicked it off. I turned it so that the barrel pointed toward the passenger seat. My finger on the trigger now. I pushed the piece until it was covered by a fold of my topcoat.

Slam of the trunk.

"It might not matter now," I said to Regina. "Who made the mistake with Ronny? You were after the stash, weren't you?"

"*He* was. I told him there wasn't a stash but he didn't believe me. He said all those old time gamblers liked to live like they didn't have two dimes to rub together."

"And you were there … when they worked on him?"

"No." A thin edge like hysteria in her voice. "I left. I got sick."

"So Falco and Tony Mitchell did the ugly work?"

"Yes." A choked tone from her, like she could not make her throat work.

"Just the three of you in it?"

"Yes, but I didn't kill anybody."

The door on the passenger side opened partly, the overhead light went on for a brief moment and then Falco slid in and closed the door behind him.

"I heard that," he said. "I'm getting tired of hearing you harp on that. It can be fixed. And maybe you ought to."

I understood the implication there. Falco couldn't be sure of Regina as long as she said things like that. The cure for it was to force her to do the job on me, or at least to do part of it. Then she couldn't pull out on him. She'd have made her bones and it would tie them together closer than a marriage certificate.

She wanted to ignore it. "Is the money all there?"

"Looks like it," he said.

"The ledger," I said. "You ran on that by accident?"

"Call it a hundred and fifty thousand dollar accident," Falco said. "The old guy, he didn't want to talk about it. He had that much loyalty. So we had to convince him."

"You must have practiced on hogs," I said.

The briefcase was across his knees, the .38 pointing at me. "Step outside," he said.

"It's cold out there. She might as well off me in here."

"Listen to the man."

"I'm not going to shoot anybody," Regina said.

"Sure you are," Falco said. "Pull the trigger once and it's over."

My finger tight over the trigger, but I didn't like the odds. He was still lined up on me and the cold iron pressed against my neck.

"Do it," Falco said.

"No." The pressure of the iron moved away from my neck. "No, I won't."

Falco said, "It's him or you, baby." The short-barrel .38 moved out of line with me, up and beyond, angling toward the back seat. I watched it, waiting my time, until the iron eye was past.

The blast of the .38 P.P. almost tore it out of my left hand. Not used to firing it with my left. I thought I'd burst my ear drums. And at the last moment maybe I chickened. It wasn't a gut shot. It hit him in the side.

Regina screamed.

I don't know how he did it. I guess he was tougher than I thought. He fell back against the door and his elbow hit the door handle. The door swung open. He kicked at me as he tumbled out. I fired again but he'd rolled toward the rear of the car as soon as he struck the asphalt.

Couldn't leave the car. Wanted to but couldn't. I shifted the iron to my right hand. I twisted around and leaned over the seat back. She was stunned, the gun in her hands but it wasn't pointed at me, and I swung my left and clubbed her on the side of her head. She bounced against the side of the car and was still. Out, I thought. I didn't have time to worry about her iron. I pushed the door handle and dropped to a knee on the asphalt. Duck walking away from the lighted car.

Falco wasn't done. He put a round into the front seat. It was from a bad angle and smashed against the dash. Might have known he couldn't reach me but he wanted me to know it wasn't a cakewalk.

And then I heard the footsteps running away. Not a steady run but like it was out of sync somehow. The shot in his side was bothering him now. I stepped around the rear of the car and started after him. He had pointed himself toward a stand of huge trees. Beyond that was a network of back lots. At that moment a car bumped over the high rise of the entrance from 8th Street. The headlights lit me up. He reached the first of the big oaks. One hand on the tree, he turned and lifted his piece. I saw the flame and took a dive for the asphalt. Another shot and that was all.

The car stopped near me and Hump was out and running, bent over, to me. He grabbed my shoulder and turned me. "You all right, Jim?"

"I was until you showed up." I stood up and ran for the car. The briefcase was still on the seat, along with the fold of xerox pages. "It's going to get busy here. Park your car. Leave the keys for me behind the visor."

I reached across the seat and punched the glove box button. I dug around and came up with the spare key. Cigarettes tumbled out. I slapped the key in Hump's hand. "Regina's in back. Check for a gun. Drive my car to my house."

"Jim ... ?"

"Meet you there."

I set out at a trot toward the network of back lots.

Twenty minutes later I gave it up. I reached 10th Street and I checked that area, all the doorways and the shops and the Society Page, a topless bar. Nothing. I came back down Peachtree, that long block between 10th and 8th. I was headed up the drive past the Follies when I saw the police cars parked there. I angled between a couple of cars and stepped down to the walk on the side of 8th Street. I walked back far enough to see that my car was gone. I stood around in a group of other curious people.

And then I walked back to Peachtree and thumbed down the first cab that cruised past. On the ride to my place, in the closed and airless cab, I got a whiff of burned cloth. I looked down at my topcoat and realized, for the first time, that I'd shot through the topcoat and ruined about a hundred and fifty dollars worth of tweed.

CHAPTER ELEVEN

"It done?" Hump sat on the sofa next to Regina Clark. The whole right side of her face, cheek and jawline, was swollen and turning dark. I guess I'd hit her a better shot than I'd meant to. At the time it hadn't seemed a good idea to play around with her hysteria and the piece she was holding.

I shucked my topcoat and showed him the burn hole just above the pocket on the right side. I tossed the coat to him and while he examined it, I got the .38 out of my waistband, swung the cylinder out and ejected the shells. I shook them around in my hand while I stared at Regina and then I opened my hand and selected the two burnt ones. I placed them on the coffee table directly in front of her. "It's done."

"Where is he?"

"Face down in a garbage can behind that picture frame house." I was talking to him but watching her out of the corner of my eye. It didn't seem to shake her any. Or maybe all the things that had happened to her in one evening had stunned her past any kind of shock.

"We close it out now?"

I thumbed shells back into the cylinder and replaced the burnt ones from the spares in my trouser pocket. "As soon as we collect the rest of the money, the other fifty thousand dollars."

Hump shifted on the sofa, his eyes lifting and fastening on Regina. "That ought to be easy."

In time it was easy. We didn't have to offer to swell the other side of her face or break an arm or leg. As soon as she really believed that Falco was dead, the dam cracked and the water ran until it was low tide.

That Sunday morning, knowing James Falco was on the list Heppler had made for me, she slipped out of Marcy's apartment and drove to Winston Place. Falco saw the danger too and they'd packed a few things and left. Falco didn't panic. He found a place and they had breakfast and he made a few calls. The money was good and it wasn't too hard to find an old corner boy who was willing to take a bit of risk for a thousand in cash.

"His name?"

"Willy Butts," she said.

"Where?"

It was an old house on Park. Willy Butts was doing some contracting now and he and a crew were replacing some sheet rock and doing some painting and plastering. For the thousand Willy took them to the house and set them up on the second floor. The original owners hadn't moved all the furniture out yet and the new owners hadn't moved in yet and wouldn't until the work was finished on the ground floor. Regina and Falco stayed in the house all Sunday and left the next morning before Butts and his crew arrived.

"And you planned to stay there tonight?"

No, they hadn't. They'd left their clothing there and they'd stashed their part of the fifty thousand, what was left after Tony Mitchell got his one third, behind the artificial gas log in the upstairs center bedroom.

"You have the key now?"

Head shaking until the movement set the pain going again in her face. "James had it."

I told Hump to mix her a strong drink. I went into the bedroom and closed the door. The Man answered the phone himself.

"What the hell has been going on? I've been waiting—"

"Take it easy. I've got the copy and the money. I've got the girl and Falco is running around out there somewhere with a hole I put in him." I took a deep breath. "Is that enough?"

"Where are you?" The Man asked. It was less a question than a demand for an answer.

"At home but I won't be here long. I found out where Falco stashed the money from the first payment. He'll head for it and, if he's hurt bad and isn't thinking straight, he might try to hole up there."

"Where?"

"Don't worry about it. I don't want your soldiers in the way."

"What are you going to do with the girl?"

"I don't know. Turn her over to Art Maloney maybe."

"That might not be wise."

"I don't feel like arguing about it right now." I didn't feel like doing much of anything. I needed about four drinks to knock me down and ten hours in bed. "Keep a tight a-hole. I'll drop the copy and the money by in an hour or so."

I hung up on him. Seconds later, about the time it would take him to find my number and dial it, the phone rang. I let it ring while I ripped the top off a fresh pack of smokes and lit one. My hand was shaking and I black-smoked half the cigarette lighting it. After twenty rings or so he gave up. I grinned at the phone, felt stupid doing it, and got my light topcoat from the closet.

Hump stood up when I entered the living room. "You're going over there by yourself?"

"Thought I might."

"I'll ride with you."

Maybe it was the way we lied all the time. He could read a lie with the best of them.

I nodded at Regina. "What about her?"

"We'll put her to bed. She needs the rest."

Hump led her into the bedroom and stretched her out on the bed while I got a roll of tape from the medicine cabinet.

I tossed the roll to him and stood in the doorway and watched while he pulled her shoes off and taped her ankles together. "I've been meaning to ask. Why did you settle on Ronny?"

"Why not? He was just another mark."

"That's rough as a cob," I said.

"You can say that. You didn't have to be pawed by him or by a hundred other men like him."

"Ronny?" I guess the shock was in my voice. "He was that way with you?"

"No, not really. But he was like those other men. He wanted it. All those fat old men who weren't any good any more, who'd offer you anything they had to suck on them to see if it'd help."

"Ronny ask that of you?"

"No, but he kept putting his fat hands on me and he kept hugging me all the time."

Hump moved to the head of the bed. He drew her right arm up and wrapped tape around the wrist. Then he taped that hand to the bedpost on that side.

"So you set him up?"

"It wasn't hard."

She knew Falco in Vegas. All the time she was acting like Ronny's long-lost daughter when he came to town. They were tight, and when Falco got in some trouble and left Vegas she wanted to join him in Atlanta. Falco was tapped-out and didn't have the airfare, so she conned Ronny for the cash. When she was in Atlanta, Falco got the idea of taking Ronny at the card table. He worked his way into Heppler's Wednesday games. But Ronny didn't open himself up in those days and Falco got the idea that he'd rob Ronny for his play money stash, the stash he knew all the big gamblers kept.

Hump circled the bed. He lifted Regina's left arm and rolled the tape around that wrist.

"As soon as you planned it, as soon as you set Ronny up, you had to know you'd have to kill him. You couldn't leave him alive."

"I didn't kill anybody," she said.

"Don't split hairs."

"All right, I knew it. But he was an old man. As far as I was concerned, he was already dead."

Hump finished with the left hand. He patted the tape end against the bedpost.

"How'd I get involved in this?" I held out my hand and Hump tossed the tape roll to me. I tore off a strip about five inches long and walked over and looked down at her.

"Ronny talked about you a time or two. He said you were getting into some shady deals and he was worried about you."

"That was all?"

Nodding. "And when I told James about you, he said you'd probably make a good middle man."

Hump stood, knees tight against the side of the bed. "It bothers me. The way you felt about Ronny, why'd you go to the memorial service?"

"Oh, it wasn't for that reason."

"Why?"

"I got curious. I wanted to see who'd be there."

I leaned over her and slapped the strip of tape across her mouth.

The door was open. No lights burning in the living room or past the high curved doorway in what was probably the dining room. A huge stack of sheetrock blocked the center of the living room. A paint-splattered tarp was spread on the floor of the dining room. The ceiling and about half the room was painted.

Light leaked down the stairs from the second floor. I moved in that direction. Hump was behind me. He wasn't carrying and I'd have to worry about him if shooting started.

Carpets on the stairs. No sound as I moved up them. A single light on the wall of the second floor hallway. Beyond that I could see the full flare of a light from a room, probably the bedroom. At the head of the stairs I stopped and listened. No sound from in there. Yes, one noise. Water running. Nothing else I could pick out.

I edged down the hall. Near the door I flattened out against the wall. Still no sound. I sucked it up and swung through the doorway. Iron up and ready. No need for that after all.

Falco was stretched out on the bed. He was bare from the waist up. He'd tried to press a towel to the wound in his side. Blood had flowed down the towel like oil follows a wick. Eyes open, blank at the ceiling. I leaned over him and felt his throat. No pulse and the skin was cold.

I looked in the bathroom. Water was running from one tap. Blood scum circled the top of the wash basin. A balled-up bloody towel was on the floor next to the tub.

I moved the fire screen and squatted. I reached behind the ceramic log and lifted out a paper-wrapped bundle. It was the right shape and feel. I tucked it under one arm and toed the fire screen back into place.

We left it exactly as it was and went down the stairs and back out to the car. I tossed the bundle into the back seat and we drove to my house.

I recognized the black who stood in the center of my living room. He was one of the two who'd picked me up that first Sunday afternoon during the ice storm aftermath. I hadn't seen any car in the drive or parked near the house.

"You walk here?"

"Got left here," he said.

I walked past him and looked through the open door at the bed. It was empty. Only a bit of tape was left at each bedpost where her hands had been.

"Where's the girl?"

"What girl? No girl here when I got here."

"What do you want?"

"The Man wants you right now."

"When I get ready," I said. I was running out of patience. The crap hitting me from all sides.

I went into the bedroom and lifted the phone receiver and began dialing. From the doorway the black moved toward me. "He said right now." I went on dialing. I got the switchboard and asked for Art Maloney.

"Yeah, Jim?"

I gave him the address on Park.

"What's there?"

"Falco. He's dead."

"You want to explain this to me? You shoot him?"

"Earlier. Down on the Strip. Found him and he took a shot at me." That was a lie but they'd have trouble proving it. I had a busted up dash to back me up.

"You going to meet me when I get there? Where are you now?"

"Out," I said. "I had the girl and she got away. I've got an idea where she might be."

"I've got to see you, Jim."

"Later," I said. I hung up and turned around and looked at the black in my bedroom doorway.

"Now I'm ready."

❧ ❧ ❧

I waited my time. First things first and then there'd be second things. I waved aside the offer of the Hines cognac and asked for a beer instead. It was PBR and had an aftertaste like swamp water.

The Man checked the Samsonite briefcase first. When he was satisfied with the stack count, he closed the top and pressed the catches home. He pushed the briefcase away and pulled the paper-wrapped bundle toward him. I hadn't bothered the tape or the paper. He ripped it away like a kid opening a Christmas present.

"It's short count," I said. "Mitchell got his share and I don't know where it is."

"One third?"

"That's what I heard."

"We'll write it off." After he approved the count, he began building a stack of tens and twenties over to one side. That completed he tapped the top of the stack with a fingernail and pushed it across the table toward me. "Five thousand. That's what I owe you, isn't it?"

I lifted the stack without counting it and passed it over my shoulder to Hump. He cracked the bundle and stuffed half into each of his topcoat pockets.

"That takes care of the business."

The Man said, "It came out better than I thought it would."

"Now I want to know where Regina Clark is."

Black hands palm down on the table top. A vein on the back of the right hand twitched. "That's not your concern anymore, Hardman."

"I think it is."

The black who'd made the ride from my house with us took that moment to step over and hand The Man the fold of xeroxed pages. The Man stripped the twine away and flipped through them.

"Vince here heard you tell Maloney that Falco is dead and that the girl got away."

I nodded. "I must have burned him worse than I thought."

"With Falco dead that solves one problem, but it leaves the girl. Think about it a minute. Think about what she could tell the police."

"She in a three foot deep hole in the woods?"

"That's too easy," The Man said.

"Here in the apartment?"

"You're welcome to look if you like."

I eased back my chair and stood up. "I'm tired of this game."

"You know what a field nigger whorehouse is?" he asked. I shook my head. "It's the last step down. It's where the busted-up ones, the ones with diseases and god knows what else, end up. Tomorrow night she'll be working in one of those houses. And she'll shake her ass and grunt with the rest of them."

"I could find her."

"Not in a year. Not in five years."

"What's to keep her from running away?"

"White powder. Smack."

"She's not a user."

"A few weeks," he said, "and she will be."

"You hate that nasty?"

Both eyes closed, he nodded. "Two years and you could pass her on the street and not know her."

It was cold and dark in the parking lot. Above me stars that were a billion or two miles away were as bright as the lamp out on the street. How small and vulnerable we are. Burning until the pale fire in us burns out.

Hump shivered and pulled his topcoat collar up. "Got to see if my car's still in the Follies lot."

I passed him the car keys and got in the passenger seat.

"You going to look for her, Jim?"

"I don't know. I'll get my head straight tonight. I'll think about it tomorrow."

"You find her," Hump said, "and they'll kill her."

"She's dead already."

Shocked at myself. Feeling the pain in my chest. I remembered where I'd heard that earlier. And it tied her to me like an anchor. I knew I could drown in it and I put my head back against the seat and closed my eyes.

Street lights fluttered against the closed lids like so many stars. Like so many white butterflies.

THE END

AFTERWORD

Ralph Dennis is The Man!
By Hank Wagner

Come along with me, and pick up your portable time machine, namely, this new edition (the original editions are even more of a time machine, smelling of old paper, and containing cigarette ads at their midpoint) of Ralph Dennis's *Hardman #7: Working for the Man*. Open it up, and travel back to Atlanta, in the early nineteen seventies, a time before CNN, competitive sports teams, or urban renewal. It's a darker, more dismal time, the perfect place for a less than heroic ex-cop named Jim Hardman to scrounge out a living doing PI work, which he makes sure to refer to as "doing favors for friends," since he doesn't have a license, and only operates under the sufferance of a pal on the force, the long-suffering Art Maloney. He doesn't pursue these somewhat squalid quests alone, though, as he is supported by his wise and knowing girlfriend, Marcy, and his partner (the original jacket text insists on calling him a sidekick, but, make no mistake, they are partners), the formidable and unflappable ex-football star Hump Evans, whose height and weight varies from book to book, always increasing.

As Hardman himself states in his all too reliable, self-deprecating narration, "Hump and I have been doing odd jobs for a couple of years. He's a lot like me. Shiftless and lazy, Marcy would say." The jobs come his way haphazardly, usually missing persons type cases, or, in this particular instance, a missing ledger, which contains information which could cripple a local gangster's operations. That gangster, a black crime lord known simply as "The Man," plays on Hardman's relationship with Ronny Gellin, a down on his luck card sharp who was murdered, apparently over the ledger. As in each of the Hardman novels, twelve in all, the truth is a bit more complicated and sordid.

I first dipped into the Hardman books in the late nineties, after hearing favorable comments from the likes of Ed Gorman, Bill Crider, and Joe Lansdale. The book scout and collector side of me was overjoyed, as I now had a quest to obtain twelve relatively obscure grails, combing my book haunts for copies of these purported gems. The reader in me was overjoyed to find out the hype was true, that Dennis was an unrecognized master of his craft, a talented journeyman writer whose work had been sadly overlooked over the years. I joyously read a handful, filing the rest away on my shelves, like fine wine, waiting for an appropriate time to revisit the mean streets of seventies Atlanta.

And along comes Lee Goldberg, who came to the books in a strikingly similar manner. Lee had much the same reaction that I did, except he took it a step further, by founding a publishing company to bring these slim volumes (the longest runs 68,000 words) back into print. He didn't get to achieve his dream immediately, but he persevered, obtaining the rights to the Dennis' literary canon (which, blessedly, extends beyond the Hardman series). You now have in your hands, or on your screen, one of those books, *Working for the Man*.

It's typical of the series, as I confirmed by dipping into an earlier book, #4, *Pimp for the Dead*, and a subsequent installment, #8, *The Deadly Cotton Heart*. *Pimp* was written in 1974, one of seven books in the series issued that year, of which *Working for the Man* was the last. *Cotton* was the first of five releases in 1976, but you'd be hard pressed to tell that any time had passed, as Dennis writes with the same skill, heart, and verve in all of them, still sticking to his formula, but doing so in a way that allowed for inventiveness and innovation along the way.

Let's go back to the time machine. *Working for the Man* was certainly a product of its time. The word "Blaxplotation" was probably just coming into use at the time, but certainly was a driving force in the marketing of this book, as witnessed by the back-cover copy, screaming in purple print, "BLACK GODFATHER." Using the term Godfather evoked Mario Puzo's 1969 novel and the 1972 film of the same name. The cover art recalls posters for the 1973 Bond film, "Live and Let Die," which featured the black super villain Mr. Big. The language he employed was often harsh and abrasive by modern standards. Neither was he afraid of presenting the South in an uncensored manner, as Hump's mere presence often evoked hateful exclamations, usually secretively mumbled by rednecks threatened by his size and confidence.

From a literary perspective, there's also much to unpack. Although the novels were marketed and packaged as men's adventure, in the vein of *The Executioner* (check out the original cover art to see exactly what I mean), prose wise, they fell somewhere between Raymond Chandler and Mickey Spillane, at least in terms of ambition and toughness. Title wise, they evoke the authors above, and the likes of the great John D. MacDonald (*The Golden Girl and All*? Come on!) They also broke some racial ground, as clear lines can be drawn from Hardman and Hump to Robert B. Parker's Spencer and Hawk (and Susan Silverman and Martin Quirk, for that matter), right through to Joe Lansdale's Hap and Leonard, a debt that Mr. Lansdale himself acknowledges in his introduction to the new edition of *Atlanta Deathwatch*. Of course, partners in mystery fiction were nothing new, but interracial partners were (I think of the Lone Ranger and Tonto as westerns, rather than mysteries). You could look to movies like 1958's *The Defiant Ones* or 1967's *In the Heat of the Night* (based on John Ball's 1965 novel), or to television shows such as *I Spy* for precedents, but the Hardman series seems to be a major turning point, at least in terms of mystery/detective literature.

In the end, I think what sold me on these books is their central character, Jim Hardman. As a younger man, I appreciated this "everyman" for his normalcy and his averageness. He was just an ordinary guy, using a specialized skill set to try to pay his rent. He wasn't above knocking back a drink or two on the job, but he never got sloppy. He was true to his girl (yet *another* word that resonates differently today), and to his partner, treating them both with respect and dignity. He always tried to keep his word. As an older man, I identify with him more than ever, as he slogs his way through his middle-aged existence, a few pounds heavier, a few steps slower, world weary and physically tired, yet still enduring, trying to use his experience and smarts to make sense of an ever more dismal world. In that way, he acts as a stand in for ordinary joes like me, making him a (an admittedly somewhat tarnished, somewhat disheveled) hero for the ages. I empathize with long time fans who are happily renewing their acquaintance with Big Jim, and envy those who are meeting him (and Hump, and Marcy, and Art) for the first time.

Hank Wagner lives in northwestern New Jersey with his wife, Nancy. A respected critic and interviewer, his work has appeared in numerous genre publications such as *Mystery Scene, Crimespree, Hellnotes, Cemetery Dance* and *Dead Reckonings.* Wagner is a co-author of *The Complete Stephen King Universe* and *Prince of Stories: A Guide to the Many Worlds of Neil Gaiman.* He also co-edited with David Morrell the Edgar, Anthony and Macavity Award finalist *Thrillers: 100 Must Reads.*

ABOUT THE AUTHOR

Ralph Dennis isn't a household name...but he should be. He is widely considered among crime writers as a master of the genre, denied the recognition he deserved because his twelve *Hardman* books, which are beloved and highly sought-after collectables now, were poorly packaged in the 1970s by Popular Library as a cheap men's action-adventure paperbacks with numbered titles.

Even so, some top critics saw past the cheesy covers and noticed that he was producing work as good as John D. MacDonald, Raymond Chandler, Chester Himes, Dashiell Hammett, and Ross MacDonald.

The *New York Times* praised the *Hardman* novels for "expert writing, plotting, and an unusual degree of sensitivity. Dennis has mastered the genre and supplied top entertainment." The *Philadelphia Daily News* proclaimed *Hardman* "the best series around, but they've got such terrible covers..."

Unfortunately, Popular Library didn't take the hint and continued to present the series like hack work, dooming the novels to a short shelf-life and obscurity...except among generations of crime writers, like novelist Joe R. Lansdale (the *Hap & Leonard* series) and screenwriter Shane Black (the *Lethal Weapon* movies), who've kept Dennis' legacy alive through word-of-mouth and by acknowledging his influence on their stellar work.

Ralph Dennis wrote three other novels that were published outside of the *Hardman* series but he wasn't able to reach the wide audience, or gain the critical acclaim, that he deserved during his lifetime.

He was born in 1931 in Sumter, South Carolina, and received a masters degree from University of North Carolina, where he later taught film and television writing after serving a stint in the Navy. At the time of his death in 1988, he was working at a bookstore in Atlanta and had a file cabinet full of unpublished novels.

Brash Books will be releasing the entire *Hardman* series, his three other published novels, and his long-lost manuscripts.